Beyond The Autumn Leaves

Jared Grace

To my children, Jordan and Wyatt.
You are always in my heart.

To my father—John Grace—I will see you again.

Reviews for *Isolation*

Jared Grace's debut novel "Isolation" is reminiscent of Stephen King's "Needful Things" where the reader navigates the inner lives, pasts, and desires of the residents of this desolate town. This story explores the darkest places of our humanity and how our history can echo into our future. Isolation shocked me and made my skin crawl, exactly what I wanted in a scary story. A great read for horror fans! ~ Kimberly Wheelock, author of Lester and Wonderland

I was drawn in from the start, so well written I could see it all as I read, almost as though I was watching a movie! (It should be a movie!) If you love a a good book and a good scare, highly recommend! Can't wait to read more from this author! 10/10 for Isolation!

World-building and character-building were exceptionally well done. This book kept me up to all hours of the morning reading I could not put it down. I highly recommend this book if you enjoy horror stories or movies. It was a fantastic job well done. Great read and a great storyteller.

I loved this book! It was the best that I've read in a long while. And I'm always reading. I felt like I was born and raised in Isolation, and that these were people that I'd known my whole life. I honestly couldn't put this book down so I didn't, I read it in a day.

Just brilliant - so pleased I stumbled across this - un-putdownable! A great mix of suspense, horror, and lore. A must-read for fans of Stephen King, Joe Hill, etc. Thoroughly looking forward to another novel by Jared Grace.

Normally, I read at bedtime; it helps me fall asleep. This book is so creepy (compliment!) that I had to switch my reading time to during daylight hours. Someone asked Jared to write a creepy, can't-fall-asleep, afraid-of-the-dark novel, and he said, "Mr King, hold my beer!" It's that good.

I loved this book! The characters are well-developed, with an easy-to-read storyline that kept me engaged! Those who follow Stephen King or Dean Koontz should give this one a read! A very well-written debut novel by Jared Grace! I can't wait to see what's next from him!

I couldn't put it down! Absolutely amazing story, great characters, kept me engaged and at the edge of my seat. I highly recommend this book to all horror novel lovers!!!

**Finalist in the 2024 Indie Ink Rewards
in the following categories.**

Best Cover
Best Setting
Best Use of Tropes
Best Light Read
Side Character MVP

Table of Contents

Chapter 1

Jesus, how long have I been driving? I thought as I drove north on Route 93 past the spattering of small cities and large trees on my way to the glorious White Mountains of New Hampshire. I looked in my rearview and realized I was the only car in sight. I let my foot press down a little harder on the gas pedal and watched as the needle on the speedometer climbed toward eighty.

I rolled down the Jeep's window and stuck my arm outside. The frigid air numbed my skin almost immediately. Goosebumps rose as though mimicking the mountains in the distance.

"Fuck it's cold," I said, forgetting the drop in temperature momentarily from my home just north of Boston to the higher elevations of New Hampshire. I rolled up the window quickly and noticed the sun beginning to rise in the east. The sun promised warmth and a truly pleasant day as I roamed in the woods. I knew that at this time of year, in New England, the cold morning air could warm up twenty or thirty degrees by lunchtime. I remember hoping that would be true that day.

The red digital numbers on the dashboard clock read 6:45 a.m.

I remember wondering what time I had even gotten up that morning. I tried to clear the cobwebs from my brain, thinking that I must have slept like shit the previous night. Not the best way to spend the night before a challenging hike. Especially a challenging hike I had never attempted before.

I rounded a bend in the highway, and Cannon Mountain came into view. Cannon Mountain, the place where the Old Man used to call home before it collapsed back in 2002, or was it 2003? Either way, now the icon of the northeast was nothing more than a memory for most and roadside attraction merchandise for all.

"Christ, my head is a mess this morning," I said to the emptiness of the Jeep. *Screw it*, I decided, as I rolled down the window again in an attempt to clear the fog.

I stuck my head slightly outside the window, and the cold slapped me across the face, shocking my system. Stinging tears rolled over my lids and were immediately blown away. I brought my head back inside and stuck my hand out of the window, letting the wind take it in an up-and-down motion, something I had done since I was a kid. My left cheek turned red as the cold continued to attack me, yet its relentless assault was doing what I had hoped—waking me up.

A shot of pain rippled through my stomach, so intense that I lurched forward in the seat. The searing burn forced my eyes shut, but only for a moment, as it dissipated as quickly as it had first appeared.

I slowly sat back in the seat, and my mind froze as I hoped that I hadn't given myself food poisoning the night before. The confusion in my head, the pain in my gut. No, I had refused to believe that was the case. I knew, somewhere inside me, that it was just my mind making up excuses to turn around and go home. I loved the woods. I loved hiking. But I hated risks. And this felt like a risk, but it was a risk I knew I had to take.

Heading into the mountains always filled me with joy beyond measure. In fact, oftentimes, I found myself like a kid on Christmas Eve night, fighting sleep with excitement brimming over inside me. That must have been why I was so groggy this morning—butterflies in my stomach before my big day.

I had planned this hike for months, years, really. I spent a lot of time in the mountains; it was my serenity—my meditative spot—but I had never tackled this trail. Going up Mount Whitehorse via the Alpine staircase was arduous but not terribly dangerous. Mount Whitehorse is a 4,800-foot mountain just southwest of the Presidential Range. I had spent months researching the trail, expected weather conditions (something that can never be truly calculated in the mountains, especially near Mount Washington, "Home to the worst weather in the world"), and average hiking time. Like I said, I never like taking risks.

Suddenly, I wondered if I'd packed well enough for this adventure. At that time, I was the type of hiker, hell maybe I always was, who would overpack for any trip, even just a short walk in the woods down the road from my house. I always planned for every eventuality in every situation so as to not be caught unaware, or surprised. So, when doing the Alpine staircase, I was going to be more prepared than usual. Why? Because eight years ago, my father had died on that very trail.

My father was an experienced hiker; he hiked for forty years. He never did any of the big mountains of the world, Everest, K2, etc., but he loved New England and what the White Mountains had to offer. He traveled out to the Rockies a couple times in his life, and while he came back with great tales of hours above the tree line and 14,000-foot peaks, he always came back to New Hampshire.

Many hikers love to track their hikes on a variety of hiking lists that can be found on the internet: the forty-eight four thousand footers, the fifty-two with a view, or if you really wanted to challenge yourself, the terrifying twenty-five. My father had completed these lists several times over, a feat he was proud to tell anyone who expressed even the slightest interest in the outdoors.

One day, over lunch, one of his buddies from work told him about Mount Whitehorse. He sold my father on the views and, considering the elevation, the relative ease of the hike. He said the trail was usually quiet because it's not on any of the lists. I remember my father coming home from work that night and telling us all about it exuberantly over the dinner table. He was shocked and wondered how he had never heard of the trail before. I remember his smile; it was infectious.

Mom, having heard a million of his hiking stories and even having gone on a few hikes herself, was excited for him. She and I were going to my grandmother's house on the day of his hike. That's the only reason we didn't go with him. I often wondered what would have happened had we been there.

He left on August 8, 2010. It was eighty-five degrees, and the sky was clear. Humidity was low. A hiker couldn't have asked for a better day. I was twenty years old.

When he didn't come home that night, Mom began to panic. Having not heard from him all day wasn't too unusual. Reception is spotty in the mountains, but when he was an hour late, then two, from his expected arrival time home, Mom called the local police. She gave them all the information she knew. She told them the mountain he was said to be hiking and the trail that he would be on.

At first, the police didn't seem too concerned. It was only a couple hours past his projected arrival time home, and any number of things could have happened: he had taken his time on the summit, the climb was a little tougher than he expected, and it was taking him longer than anticipated, hell, maybe he had a flat tire. There were any number of reasons he could be late. I remember sitting on the couch, even then not overly concerned, listening to my mother pleading with the police to drive over to the trailhead and at least check to see if his car was still there. It was as though she knew.

Reluctantly, they sent an officer to the trailhead and found my father's car still parked where he had left it hours before. The officer, having little to do in this area of rural New Hampshire that night, parked his car next to my father's and waited. As darkness began to fall and my father had still not returned, the officer started to get a little anxious about the situation also. He called in Fish and Game and, along with a few volunteers from the area, discussed the situation in the parking lot. With no call for help and, with the exception of the darkness creeping in, ideal trail conditions, they felt they had little to worry about.

The crew of five volunteers and one Fish and Game officer made their way up the trail, headlights bobbing up and down as they marched up The Staircase. The officer later told us that they found my father about two miles up. The Staircase flattens out for about a quarter of a mile in an area known as Hiker's Rest. At this point, you've climbed about 2,500 vertical feet, all of which is, yup, you guessed it, a granite staircase. With another 1,500 feet of vertical elevation to go, Hiker's Rest is where most will stop to grab a snack and rest their weary legs.

Hiker's Rest is scattered with flat rocks, about waist high (depending on the height of the hiker, of course), that allow for a perfect bench to sit on. As you ascend, off to the right, a few yards into the woods, there is a steep slope that leads to a waterfall about sixty feet below. Steep is perhaps an understatement. It's almost vertical, with several small outcrops on the way down that make any ascent or descent almost impossible to manage. But the views from the top of the ledge are breathtaking. White water cascades over a thirty or forty-foot drop and continues on as far as the eye can see. For thousands of years, the water has poured over those rocks. I always thought the flow of time utterly amazing. The noise is thunderous throughout most of the year, but it is certainly the best spot on the trail to sit and enjoy nature.

To the left of Hiker's Rest is a lush, vivid landscape. The trees are thick, and the grasses and ferns create an ocean of green that stretches on forever. When the river is running slow, and the sound is a bit muted, you can stare off into this section of forest and hear eternity echoing back.

As the years passed and the pain of losing my father started to subside a little, I convinced myself that there was some comfort in knowing that he had died in such a beautiful place. But really, that only helps to put a bandage on a gaping wound. Sure, his last sight may have been beautiful, but he's still gone. And that pain never fully heals. Someone once said to me that you never know when the last time you'll hold someone is. The last time you'll kiss someone. The last time you'll hear their voice. But one day, that last time will come, and your memories will be all that you have left.

One of the rescuers told me later that Dad was found—face down—at the precipice of the cliff at Hiker's Rest. His body had been off the trail, but his green pack with those vibrant red straps stood out. God, he always loved that pack.

He hadn't passed too long before they got there. He looked peaceful, the rescuer told me.

They did an autopsy, and they found that he had died of a heart attack. Dad kept in shape. He had a bit of a sweet tooth, but overall ate well and exercised regularly. When he died, I realized to live a happy and safe life, I needed to make sure I did everything I could to minimize risk. I figured it maximized life expectancy, and the longer your life, the more chances you have to experience it. Oddly enough, the only time I felt like I could take a risk or two (usually minor ones) was out on the trail. Maybe that was a bit of Dad coming out of me.

I kept driving through Franconia Notch at a steady pace, still not a car in sight. Cannon Mountain, with its gigantic rock face, loomed over the Jeep. Driving through the notch always made me feel claustrophobic. On either side, the mountains stare menacingly down upon you. The mountains themselves aren't evil or wicked, but an overwhelming feeling comes from them nonetheless. It's almost like watching a mouse scurry past your feet while you're in your kitchen. You're not a mean-hearted person, but you want to be rid of that mouse. That's what being in the notch feels like. Like you're being tolerated, but you'll only be tolerated for as long as you're permitted.

Why are you here, little being? You can stay, but respect us, or we will strike you down.

I had smirked in the driver's seat and snickered just slightly at the thought of some rock face staring down from above with a scolding look.

"I will respect your space, Mr. Mountain," I remember joking.

I took my exit and drove the backroads toward Mount Whitehorse. The road is narrow, and the density of the trees is staggering here. How any big game could find its way through there always boggled my mind.

Off in the distance, a moose crossed the road, slowly and majestically. I slowed the truck a distance away, careful not to startle the animal. His fur was glistening from the morning dew that had saturated it. Under the fur, muscles rippled, and the power of nature once again overwhelmed me. Sturdy and prideful, the moose lowered its head and pushed its way into the dense thicket on the other side of the road.

For a moment longer, I kept the truck idling in the middle of the road. It was still so early, and the road remained empty as far as my eyes could see. When the moose disappeared fully into the darkness, I finally took my foot off the brake and allowed the truck to continue to my destination. Mount Whitehorse was only just down the road.

Somewhere in my mind, I could remember my father telling me about the animals of the forest and what they can represent to us. I clearly remembered the moose represented courage when facing a difficult task.

Fitting, I thought. *Maybe this is Dad giving me a sign that I can do this.* At least, that's what I wanted to believe.

The final few miles passed quickly as I turned my truck left onto the dirt road that led to the trailhead. Going any faster than a slow crawl was not wise here, even with the Jeep set several feet off the ground. The road was dug up, and the holes that lived there were deep and sharp. *A good way to blow a tire.*

As the sun rose higher in the sky, the leaves began to show their true beauty. The cold, crisp nights had sped up the metamorphosis that takes place every year in these woods. The forest, in the summer lush and green, changes to a polychromatic display of the most beautiful colors imaginable.

Autumn in New England was always my favorite season. It is and will always be the number one reason why I never wanted to permanently leave. Even as a kid, when my family would take us north, sometimes to Lincoln but more often to North Conway, I would stare out the window and imagine the leaves falling all around me. A rainbow of color collecting over me. The leaves, cold to the touch, sending a chill throughout my body, exhilarated me.

When we would arrive at our destination I would spend the first few moments scanning the area, looking for the largest and most beautiful leaf I could find. I'd find that leaf and keep it by my side for the length of our trip. I knew it wouldn't keep forever, and eventually, it would become stiff and crumble at the slightest touch, but even in the final moments of its existence, I would hold it to my nose and smell the earthy, satisfying scent that it held.

Driving down the dirt road I found myself feeling that same sense of wonder that I felt as a child. The trees felt otherworldly. They looked much like a child's painting, casting varying colors over the canvas in ways that didn't seem to make sense at first but held beauty and wonder that only a fantastical imagination could come up with. I noticed gooseflesh once more covering my arms and a smile, large and true, appearing on my face as I pulled into the first parking spot I came upon.

Once more, I saw no other cars around. *Not surprising,* I thought. *I must have got lucky today, no one to share the trail with.* As I opened my door and stepped outside, the satisfying sound of my boots crunching against the dirt pleased me. It had been too long since I had enjoyed the company of the trees and the silence they brought. I opened the back door of the Jeep and took out my pack—my father's pack. The pack he took on every hike, including his final one.

Over the years, people had told me this was a bit morbid. That I should get a new pack that hadn't been part of the untimely passing of my old man. Bad juju, most would say. But I found comfort in the pack. My father was the closest person to me and carrying this with me allowed me to bring a piece of him on my adventures.

When I was alone, speaking to him on the trail, I knew he could hear me if I had his pack strapped to me. As I went over my mental checklist of all the things I may need, I marveled at how rugged the pack looked. Worn in some places, dirt covered in even more, but sturdy and reliable.

Sturdy and reliable, just like Dad. He'd be with me today.

I hoisted the red straps over my shoulders and secured the pack snugly against my body. I took a sip from my water bottle and stood at the mouth of the trailhead.

4.5 miles to Mount Whitehorse summit, it read in bold letters carved into the worn wooden sign.

I imagined my dad standing here, not knowing it would be the last time he would set foot on a trail. Not knowing he had already kissed my mother for the last time. Not knowing we had already spoken our last words to each other.

I took a deep breath and held it in, releasing it slowly after several seconds.

Then I stepped onto the trail.

Chapter 2

Mom had a really hard time after Dad passed. When she was asked to come down to the hospital to identify the body, she collapsed on the living room floor, wailing and screaming. Her words wouldn't come. I was there that night, the memory of laying on the floor forever burned into my consciousness. I knelt next to her and wrapped my arms around her, pulling her close. I didn't know what else to do.

She sobbed, her head buried against my chest, for what felt like hours. I can still remember how the blue of my shirt darkened as it soaked in her tears. I spoke no words; sometimes silence is best. My words didn't come, not simply because I thought it was the best choice, but because my world was collapsing around me as well. The feeling of unreality was overwhelming. My mother's heaving body was the only thing that kept me grounded.

How was it possible that I would never hear his voice again? That we'd never watch a game together again? When I woke up that same morning, I had heard him laughing in the kitchen with my mother. It felt like a dream. No, a nightmare.

When she finally composed herself, I asked if she was ready to go down to the hospital. She said that she was, and we slowly made our way out to the car, knowing our lives were about to change forever. Though in reality, we knew they already had. I remember holding her against my body as we slowly made our way out into the warm night. The crickets, they sounded so damn loud. I wonder why I remember that now.

Why is it that whenever you are sad, the radio only seems to play sad songs? It's like the universe is making sure you can hit the deepest depths of sorrow so that you can embrace the rise to the highest heights. My mother stared out the passenger window, silent for the entire ride. I wished she had talked to me during that drive—or held my hand—or showed me some sort of comfort. Is that selfish?

I went into the room with her to identify my father's body. I was frozen. Not just physically. It was as though time stood still. As they pulled back the sheet and exposed his face, my mother brought her hands to her own. She sobbed quietly into them. I walked slowly over and placed my hand on his chest.

It was real. He was gone.

Time passed, as it always does, and normalcy slowly started to return to our lives.

I decided to stay at my parents' house with my mother for a little longer to make sure her adjustment to life without Dad was as natural as it could be. To be honest, I stayed for my own well-being, also. Being in the house I grew up in, the place where Dad had spent the last of his days, felt right. I didn't want to leave, though I knew one day I would.

I cried only once through the whole experience. Just once. Isn't that strange? It was after we came back from the hospital. Mom went and lay down in her room, and I went to mine. I pulled out my cell phone and was looking at my text messages. I pulled up the last text conversation I had with him. We were arguing. Not about anything serious, but we argued. It wasn't even the last conversation I had with him, but it hit me like a heavyweight fighter's right hook to the gut. I rolled onto my stomach and cried like a baby into my pillow.

Months passed, and spring rapidly approached. The trees began to bud, and the animals started coming out of whatever place they called home. I was preparing to move out of the house and into my own apartment a few towns away. Far enough to find my independence but close enough to come back home anytime Mom (or I) needed it. Spring is a time of change, the start of something new. It felt right to start my own personal journey then.

It was still early in the morning, no later than eight or nine, when Mom knocked on my bedroom door. She pushed the door open when I beckoned her to come in. Her eyes danced around the room at the boxes laying everywhere, the walls barren of all the posters, pictures, and memories that they once held. I could see the emotion wash over her, but she kept her composure.

"Matt," she said softly before raising her eyes to look at me, "let's get out of the house. Let's go take a hike. Just something small. Like we used to do with Dad."

I looked around the room at what I had left to do before I set out on my own. I hadn't been out on any trail since Dad died, and the invitation staggered me with an intensity I wasn't prepared for. "I don't know, Mom. I still have a lot to do and…"

She held her hand up to cut me off before I could make any number of excuses as to why I couldn't find the time. "Matt, you've stayed here longer than I know that you intended. You're leaving in a couple of days to finally begin your life. I'm afraid to go out into the woods again without your father, too, but if you're starting a new chapter yourself, let's fully close the last one."

She took another step into my room and let her eyes wander to the place where a picture of the three of us once rested. I followed her gaze, and my heart sank, fully understanding what she was thinking.

"We'll take a drive up to Mount Willard, your dad's favorite, and we'll say one final goodbye," she prodded. She could see I was still slightly hesitant but didn't need much more of a nudge to be convinced. "We'll stop at your favorite burger place on the way back. You know, the one in Lincoln."

I smiled and told her I'd meet her downstairs shortly.

As I changed into my hiking clothes, I realized that I needed this as much as she did. In only a few days, she'd be coming home to a silent house for the first time in twenty-one years. She'd eat dinner alone for the first time. She'd sit by the TV trying to ignore the silence and the sadness that was threatening to take over, alone for the first time. When she turned out the lights to go to bed, she'd be alone in the house, knowing no one would be coming home for the first time.

But I knew that I would be having the same experiences. The difference was, my book would be in the exposition phase, while I thought Mom felt like her book was in the falling action sequence, rapidly heading for the conclusion. Of course, Mom likely had many pages in front of her before her book was closed, but change can be difficult at any point in life; our thoughts can fall into a deep hole if we allow them to.

I came downstairs to find Mom outside with our backpacks set up against the car. "Let's go, slowpoke. I've already got everything packed." She got in the driver's seat and started the car. I tossed the packs in the trunk before taking my position as co-pilot as we drove off to Mount Willard.

It was not even lunchtime when we rounded the corner that led to the parking lot at the Crawford Notch Highland Center. We both were expecting the cars to be overflowing from the small lot and down the side of US-302. On bad weather days, this is often the case, but today, even with the sun shining and the birds singing, there were only a couple of cars parked in the dirt lot.

What luck, I thought, and Mom must have read my mind because she said, "I can't believe it either."

We got out of the car and grabbed our packs, took a sip from our water bottles, and headed toward the bathrooms just before the trailhead. Dad always said, "When you're hiking with a woman, always be sure to stop at an *actual* bathroom before you get on the trail. And while you're there, you might as well go, too."

I finished first and stepped back out into the parking lot, looking across US-302 toward the small lake that was in the foreground to the high peaks of the Presidential range in the distance. As the sun beat down upon it, the ice was slowly melting on the lake. When the cars were not driving past, if you listened closely, you could hear the frozen lake moving beneath. This was a sight and a sound I would never tire of. When the road is busy, and dozens of hikers are preparing for their day in the lot, this scene could be lost in the hustle and bustle, but if you have quiet surrounding you, it is easy to become lost in its beauty.

I must have been fully engrossed because when Mom came up behind me and put a hand on my back, I was startled and whipped my head around quickly. She laughed and asked me if I was ready to go. I took one final look at the lake and nodded. "One more trip up. For Dad," I said. Mom smiled.

Mount Willard is a fairly gradual hike. Shortly after you enter the woods, you'll take a left at the fork in the trail. The trail is flat for a short distance, though you do have to hop over a few small stream crossings. Dad brought me here countless times as a child, and I would always get a kick out of walking right through the water, which was normally not deep enough to get me too wet. After the second stream crossing the trail rises steadily for about a half mile. At this point, you come to a small waterfall that has been given the name "Centennial Pool." Neither Mom nor I had been out on the trail for quite a while, so we decided to take a short break there and watch the water pour over the small drop and crash against the rocks below. Our breath was already coming in deeply and rapidly.

Mom sat on one of the flat rocks that had called this place home for as long as time existed. I chose to sit on the ground. We drank from our water bottles and had some peanut butter crackers but spoke no words. We just listened to the water flowing and the quiet sound of the birds singing, dampened by the crashing of the water—one with nature.

We only sat for a few minutes (you don't want to sit for too long, or you'll run the risk of getting stiff and having a very uncomfortable day) before we continued on our trek. We followed the trail up and up, gradually gaining elevation. We passed a pine tree that had been cut, the overwhelming smell of Christmas flooded our nostrils. Mom and I both agreed that there may be no better smell in the world.

As we climbed higher, the wind began to pick up slightly, and the forest began to open up a bit more. We had hiked this trail so many times before that we knew we would be reaching the summit soon. Up one more small rise, and at the end of the trail was an opening in the trees. We had made it. I stopped and let Mom walk out onto the summit first.

After spending the last hour amongst the trees, the views from the summit were breathtaking. Mom's breath caught, and she placed a hand to her mouth. I stepped out just behind her and placed a hand on her back. I remembered the first time I had seen the view with my dad—Crawford Notch, opening up before your eyes. Cars, like tiny ants, driving by hundreds of feet below. To the left, Mount Webster and the southernmost point of the Presidential mountains, Mount Jackson. To the right, the trio of Mount Willey, Mount Field, and Mount Tom. And straight ahead countless mountains, all of which my dad had promised to conquer one day. Many of which he did.

Somehow, we were the only two on the summit that morning. How we found ourselves that lucky was a mystery that will always remain unsolved. Perhaps, somewhere out there, Dad played a part in that miracle.

Mom walked out to the edge of the cliff that plummets hundreds of feet to the street and the railroad tracks below. She sat down hard on the granite summit and cried. I stood behind her and allowed myself to cry for my father for only the second time. Neither of us looked at the other, both of us in our own minds remembering the man he was and what he meant to us. After a while, both of our tears stopped, and I sat next to Mom.

Still, we sat in silence and took in the view. The sun shone on our faces, keeping us warm even while the wind blew off of Mount Washington. A pair of small gray jays chirped and flew around us, curious if we were going to offer them any of our food. We did not. Below us, the train passed, and we watched as it traveled into the trees and out of sight. Modernity being swallowed by timelessness.

As we heard voices approaching from behind us, my mother turned to me. "You ready to go grab a burger?"

I nodded and said that I was. I began to walk toward the mouth of the woods again and stopped when I realized she was still staring off into the distance. I watched her, a woman in her early fifties about to start her life over, and realized she'd be okay. She was a tough woman and a loving woman. She'd be okay. We both would.

As she turned and walked past me I found myself now staring out at the splendor of the world seen from a vantage point unrecognizable to the drivers below. I saw Dad standing at the edge of the cliff. I saw myself as a child, having chosen a "picnic rock," as Dad had called it, near the edge, but not too close, where we sat and ate our snacks. I saw him put his arm around me, and I smiled.

"Love you, Dad."

Chapter 3

I'd been hiking for an hour, or was it two? I always looked at the time before I got on the trail. It helped me gauge my pace, which is just a small statistic I like to keep in mind when I'm out there. Of course, I would forget to do that. Crappy night of sleep, cobwebs in my head all morning, being on the trail where my father died. *I can give myself a pass today on the small mistakes*, I thought.

The trail was rugged. What started as a really easy first quarter of a mile quickly turned into an almost vertical ascent up the Alpine Staircase. I stopped several times to take in the view (at least that's what I was telling myself) and drink some water (gotta stay hydrated, another mantra I kept repeating). My legs were absolutely burning, but I kept telling myself not to sit. *You'll stiffen up, and then you really won't be able to finish this.*

Every hiker, no matter your experience level, has a lazy voice that speaks within his or her head once the going has gotten tough for some time. That voice that questions every step. That voice that tells you that you can't finish. That voice that just wants to be on the couch binging Netflix and drinking a beer. My lazy voice had started to creep into my head, quietly at first but getting progressively harder to ignore. Whenever my lazy voice got too loud, I would simply remind myself that the view from the top was worth it, and when I got back to the car, I could head right to the closest pizza spot and get a greasy pepperoni pizza as a reward.

"Hiking is a head game and you can't let the lazy voice win," one of Dad's favorite sayings.

Determined to see how much time I'd been out on the trail, and maybe more importantly at that moment, how much more time I could expect to spend on this damned staircase, I pulled out my phone to get my bearings.

"Dead," I said frustratingly. "Well, isn't that just great?"

I held down the power button, thinking that perhaps it had simply turned off and just needed to be restarted; no such luck. Ultimately, I decided that it wasn't a big deal. The Alpine Staircase is one single trail; no way to get lost; just keep putting one foot in front of the other. So, that's what I decided to do.

The birds sang beautiful ballads amongst the trees. I could pick out the sounds of chickadees, warblers, and thrush. Listening to them slowed my breathing, and I found myself getting into a rhythm to match their calls. There was no movement in the trees, just the calls of the morning and maybe the warning that someone was spoiling their privacy.

When my legs felt like they couldn't take another step, I saw a flattened area appear before me. The sound of water, audible somewhere in the back of my mind for a while, took the forefront and drowned out the sound of the birds. With a final push, knowing that I could finally sit down, I found myself off the staircase and onto Hiker's Rest.

The intensity of the staircase was good for one thing, keeping my mind off of where I was heading and why I was going there. Now that I was there, emotion overwhelmed me. I sat on the closest flat-topped rock, a huge piece of granite that had been left here eons ago by some receding glacier, and tried to catch my breath. *In through your nose, out through your mouth.*

The river sounded thunderous below. It was autumn in the mountains, yet the rivers were still running high. I glanced over to the spot that was described to us, where my father had fallen, and quickly averted my eyes. Sadness, awe, and a stabbing pain in my heart wouldn't allow me to take in the scene. Not quite yet.

I peeled off my backpack and set it down next to me. I looked at the amount of gear that I had brought and shook my head. No wonder this was so difficult. I had forty pounds strapped to my back—a tent, sleeping bag, and even crampons. What was I thinking? I was making this so much harder on myself. *Preparing for anything is one thing, but you really need to pull it back some,* I thought.

I reached into the pack and took out some peanut butter crackers and one of my bottles of water. I always hated bringing plastic bottles into the woods. It felt like I was cheating on Mother Nature, but the convenience factor often won out. I looked over my shoulder to see where I had come from. The steepness was impressive, and I felt proud that I was finally doing what I had planned to do for years.

I realized that Hiker's Rest felt a bit like the Centennial Pool on Mount Willard, where I had shared snacks and water with my mother and father in years past. The water roared louder, and the drop was far more precipitous, but sitting on the rocks and listening to the cascade brought nostalgia to my heart. I smiled and thought of my father sitting in this same spot. I wondered what he was thinking here, on his last day.

I steeled myself enough to look over to the flat patch of grass that was near the edge of the cliff that led down to the waterfall and river below. "Here's to you, Dad," I said as I lifted my bottle of water in a salute.

I sat a bit longer than I wanted, and when I rose to put on my pack and begin my summit push, I had to stretch my legs and back. I pushed against a tree close by to stretch out my hamstrings and quads. I put my foot at an angle against one of the stones, stretched out my Achilles heel, and reached down as far as I could to open up my back. I was ready to go.

As I pulled the red straps across my shoulders, I realized the insanity of carrying this much weight when, in all likelihood, I could summit the mountain and be back down to Hiker's Rest within an hour and a half, two max. It was a risk, and I didn't like the idea of being without any gear should I need it, but I calculated the options in my head and decided leaving the weight behind and making a strong push to the summit outweighed the fear.

I placed the pack against the rock that I had been sitting on, grabbed a bottle of water and a small bag of trail mix to enjoy at the summit, and began my trek once again. Instantly, I noticed the difference in my pace and energy level. My legs weren't burning nearly as much as they had been, and my lungs didn't feel as though they were going to burst out of my chest at any moment. *Leaving the pack was a good idea*, I thought.

The trees started to become more stunted the further I went. The forest that I started within had changed before my eyes. Trees that stood one hundred feet tall in some areas now reached only about twenty. Moss spread across the forest floor. The lush green radiated in the sun. It looked like the most plush carpet in the world. The temptation to leave the trail entirely and go lay upon it was fierce, but I had a goal to complete.

Once I passed the mattress of green, the trees faded away entirely. The sun shone above and dried the sweat from my shirt, warming my bones. There was not a cloud to be found in the crystal blue sky. The colors seemed so radiant. *Dad's here,* I thought. The wind had died down as I broke tree line, leaving only a slight breeze to cool my face. I continued to climb. Determination and the emotion of being where my dad had been drove me onward.

Abruptly, I was there. It came upon me so unexpectedly that I had to look around to be sure it wasn't a false summit. The bald summit of Mount Whitehorse was beneath my feet. I found myself completely overjoyed and overwhelmed to be standing where I was. I was sad to know this was the last mountaintop view my dad ever saw. But I was glad that it was the beauty that I beheld in front of me.

I sat down and closed my eyes, letting the slight breeze and warmth of the sun wash over me. The world around me began to fade away, and I thought of everything that had led to this point. I thought of my father's passing; I thought of my mother, her strength when he passed, and her strength tested again when I left home; I thought of Jane when I first met her at the high school I was teaching at. She was fresh out of college, the woman that would one day be my wife. The sadness of her miscarrying, the joy of trying again, and having a healthy little girl. It felt like all the good in life and the struggles as well led to this point. I conquered my fears, pushed past my comfort zone, and found myself triumphantly here, in this moment.

I opened my eyes finally and looked at the panoramic view of all the mountains around me. To my right, the snow-capped peaks of the Presidential range, highlighted by Mount Washington, standing prominently above all others. Even at the height at which I found myself, "The Rock Pile" felt like it loomed over me. Behind me, and slightly to my left, the mountains of Lafayette and Lincoln that make up the wondrous Franconia Ridge Trail. I remembered reading in National Geographic that it was on the list of the most beautiful hikes in the country. I made a mental note to make sure to conquer that hike next.

And straight ahead of me, far off to the north, stood a little mountain, maybe even a large hill, that seemed to give off a strange ambiance. Even at this distance, the hill seemed to carry a story with it.

With some effort, I peeled my eyes away from the beauty that stood before me and rose from my seat at the summit. I had finished my snack and hydrated myself enough to begin my journey back. Besides, leaving my pack, my dad's pack, at Hiker's Rest was starting to give me a bit of anxiety. I needed to make sure it was still safe and accounted for before I could truly let everything I had accomplished sink in.

I took one last deep breath, enraptured by the crisp mountain air, and spoke a quiet word of thanks for being allowed to experience this moment. I imagined my dad standing in this very spot, a smile prominent on his face. I turned back toward the trail and headed back from whence I came.

As the wind blew past my ears, I thought I heard a voice calling my name. I turned back to the summit but saw nothing but a swirling cloud of dirt, kicked up by the breeze. I shrugged and kept on my way, feeling the gaze of a familiar energy all around me.

My heart soared.

Chapter 4

When I was fifteen years old, my dad and I set out on our first trail on the *Terrifying 25* list. These hikes are not all long or even necessarily high in elevation, but they all have sections that can be described as…well, terrifying.

We decided to do the Morgan and Percival trail in Holderness, New Hampshire. A small town that sits on Squam Lake in the central region of New Hampshire, Holderness gives off that classy small-town-New England feel. This particular trail, only about a five-mile loop, seemed completely within my capabilities, though even then, I treated life with a sense of caution. So, even while I knew I could physically do it, the term "terrifying" scared me to death.

I think that was the reason he suggested it.

Much about this trail is anything but terrifying. It certainly has its steep sections, but, for the most part, you enjoy a scenic trail in the middle of the woods with nothing too arduous in front of you. Until you are just about to reach the summit of Mount Morgan. At this point, you must scale three ladders that rise about thirty feet above. But, for me, it might as well have been a thousand feet.

The first two ladders are just a normal hand-over-foot climb. But on the third ladder, you must reach out over a gap and grab a hold before swinging yourself over open air and continuing the climb into and through a small cave. I had never done anything like that before. I seriously considered taking the trail that leads around the ladders a short way off.

Dad wouldn't hear of it. He wanted me to overcome my fear. To take a risk, one that he deemed small even if I saw it as a potentially life-altering decision. He climbed first, and I watched, sweat covering every inch of my body. I thought about how I would be able to hold on to the wooden ladders well enough to cross the gap with my palms as sweaty as they were. I watched as he made it onto the third ladder with ease and called to me from the safety of the small cave above. I felt sick, but I didn't want to let him down.

I took the first two ladders rung by rung, slowly—carefully. When I reached the gap, I thought there was no way I could do it. I made the mistake that everyone makes. I looked down and got dizzy. I leaned into the ladder and closed my eyes, willing any courage that I had to show itself. Then I heard my dad above me, looking down from the top of the third ladder. He told me that I could do it, that the sense of accomplishment when I was on the other side would be worth it.

I don't know that I believed him, but I reached over nonetheless, grabbed the third wooden ladder, and swung myself onto it. I scrambled to the top of it and into the cave. Dad was laughing, and after a moment's pause, I fell into laughter as well. I did it. I think it was at that moment that I realized that calculated risks in the woods were something I could be comfortable with, even if not out in the *real* world.

After the cave was a short scramble to the summit. A picturesque view of Squam Lake greeted us. As I stood there and looked out at the world beneath, I had the same sense of wonder as I always did when I was on top of a mountain, but this time, it was multiplied by the exhilaration I felt as my body had swung over the precipice below the ladders. Dad put his arm around me, and we sat in silence.

We shared the summit that day with half a dozen other people, but we found a spot away from many of them where we could talk. This is where my dad imparted some of his wisdom to me. Be a hard worker. Fight for what you believe in. Treat women with respect. Chivalry isn't dead. And perhaps most importantly, live every day as if it were your last. I realized as we headed off toward Mount Percival, to complete our hike that the moment we shared on the summit of Mount Morgan, overcoming the fear he knew I'd have, that was why he wanted a father-son day. He wanted to show me how to trust myself. He wanted me to see on my own—without him having to tell me—that if I believed in myself, I could accomplish anything.

I thought about that day often after he passed. That was one of the most special days of my life.

Chapter 5

Still riding the high from completing my trek and spending time on the summit in my father's footsteps, I approached Hiker's Rest once more.

As I got within a few yards from where I had sat a short while ago, panic took hold of my mind.

"Where is my pack?" I said to the silence of the woods. I had placed it against the rock in which I had sat, but now only flattened grass greeted me. I ran to the rock and got on my knees, as though the bag had somehow sunk into the ground and getting lower to the grass would reveal its evil trick.

As I knelt in the flattened grass, I looked down the trail, sure some hiker had seen a pack with no owner to claim it and thought it a treasure trove of hiking goodies. *Why did I always pack so damn much?* I chastised myself. I rose from my knees and sat back on the rock once more, head in hand.

I cursed myself mentally. How could I lose my pack? How could I lose my *father's* pack? If I had just born the weight a little longer, I wouldn't have had to leave it here. "Stupid, stupid, stupid," I said as I looked toward the place in which my father's body was found.

In my agitated state, I hadn't thought to look all around me. I was so sure the pack was lost that I didn't turn my head to see it lying only a few yards away…where my father had been found.

Utter confusion overtook me. I knew the pack was left against the rock, yet it lay resting away from where I had placed it. I looked around for animal tracks and saw none. I scanned once more for signs of human tracks and once again was left mystified. My mind swirled with explanations, but none made any sense. A chill crept over my body as I felt something strange overcome the area.

I decided the mystery of the moving backpack could wait to be solved until I made it back to the trailhead. As I walked over to retrieve the pack, I stopped momentarily with it at my feet. I looked down at the water that cascaded over the rocks below. The water moved fast, its immense power filling me with awe the longer I stared at it from my elevated position. My head began to swim as the hypnotic movement of the deluge mesmerized me. I rocked back and forth slightly and needed to reach out to steady myself against a nearby tree.

I finally drew my eyes away and bent over to retrieve the curious moving pack when I had an overwhelming sense of a presence behind me. The same feeling I felt on the summit a little while previous. I raised the pack slowly and put it on my shoulders, paying attention to every noise I could hear over the rumbling water. I hesitated to turn, sure there was a great beast behind me. A black bear, perhaps even a moose. *I'd rather it be the bear,* I thought as I steeled my resolve, ready to fight for my life.

I turned slowly. The sun shone through the trees, causing rays of light to dance in my sight line. When I turned entirely around, I saw the figure of a man standing in front of me. *It must be the person who moved my pack. But why?* I raised my eyes to greet the person behind me when horror struck my heart.

"Matt," my father's raspy, phantasmal voice spoke as he reached out a hand to touch me.

A shockwave of terror struck me as I stepped away from the familiar figure in front of me. When my right foot slipped past the edge of the cliff, my pack pulled me over.

The last sight that I saw before crashing into the freezing water below was my father looking down at me, his arms stretched out, reaching out to save me.

Chapter 6

For just a moment, my stomach felt as if it was in my throat. A free fall unlike the drop on a roller coaster; there was nothing holding me tight, keeping me safe. My vision became pinpoints that focused only on the man who appeared to be my father, holding his hands out to me. Reaching out from beyond the grave to save me. Did he end up killing me instead?

Time slowed as I fell. I tried to convince myself that it could not have been my father. It was only a man that resembled him. It had to be. But how would a stranger know my name? Was it written somewhere on my pack? But the voice, it was his voice. It had to be him, but how?

The smack of my body hitting the water was nothing compared to the intense shock of being submerged in the near-freezing temperature. I succumbed to the numbness that overwhelmed me. My eyes were shut, and being immersed in the water, floating weightlessly, gave me a surreal sense of flying through time. I could feel nothing. I could hear nothing more than the small, trapped bubbles of air floating by me as I rushed down the raging river.

My knee smacked against a rock hidden below the surface of the torrent.

My immediate instinct was to scream, yet when I sucked in air to generate the yell, I found only water filling my lungs. My eyes snapped open, and panic overtook me again as I looked, disoriented, into the water. I couldn't tell which way brought me above the surface and which way would bring me to a watery grave. I had no choice but to kick my feet and swing my arms in the direction that I thought would offer me safety.

Just as I felt myself beginning to black out, my head surfaced. The water stung my eyes and blurred my vision. Colors flashed before me, but whether they were the sky, man, or animal, I couldn't say.

I began coughing. River water and bile spewed from my mouth. My stomach tightening below the surface made it impossible for me to continue kicking my legs to stay afloat, so I waved my arms harder. The numbness worked its slow torture on my extremities and slowed my arms with each passing second. My head spun as I was rushed further and further away from the cliff from which I fell. My vision faded once more, and my head once again sank beneath the torrent.

The last thought I had was an acknowledgment that this is what it was like to die.

My eyes slowly opened. I was lying in the mud, half in the river and half out. I was frozen to the bone. My clothes were soaked and clung to my body as I shimmied forward, desperate to get my lower body out of the river. I could hardly raise my head as my chin dragged through the mud. The freezing muck pooled against my face with each desperate inch I crawled forward. When my feet were out of the soaking river and fully onto the only slightly soaking ground, I allowed myself to collapse onto my chest once more.

I lay there, chilled to the bone and shivering uncontrollably. I couldn't feel my hands or my feet, the latter of which was currently residing in flooded boots. The urge to give in to the sleep that threatened to overtake me was immense. Somewhere in the back of my mind, I knew that if I was shivering, then my body was doing the right thing. I was still alive.

My breath steamed from my mouth and caressed my fingers. The warmth coated them, and the sensation of ice melting along my knuckles sent my head spinning. Tingles, first dull then sharp like pinpricks, worked their way from the tips of my fingers to the palm of my hand; I breathed harder against them, fighting through the pain. I flexed my fingers slowly, thumb to pinky, one at a time, urging the blood to flow. As I did that with my left hand, I rotated my head and began breathing hard on my right, the left side of my face that had stayed fairly clean now lying in the mud.

My toes worked in the same pattern until the blood began flowing in them as well. Warmth continued up my legs and down my arms until I was able to bend my arm at the elbow and test my strength. I needed to get out of the mud and get my clothes off—start a fire. Once I managed to get on all fours and get my core out of the mud, I was shocked to find the ease with which I was able to stand. I gave myself a mental check for pain emanating from anywhere. Surprisingly, other than being bitterly cold, I found myself to be uninjured.

I walked a few steps away from the shore and saw the green and red pack sitting a few yards away against a tree. "How the…" I exclaimed as I hustled toward it, peeling my shirt off as I went. I picked up the pack, shivering, and realized that it was completely dry. There was not a speck of mud or dirt on it either. "But, how…"

A chill ran up my now topless body, and I snapped back to reality, knowing I needed to get warm, and fast. I placed the pack at its previous resting spot and pulled off my boots. A wave of river water poured out of one and then the other.

When I was stripped down to nothing, I searched my pack for warm clothes. I put them on as quickly as I could, the dry clothes feeling heavenly against my still-frozen skin. I ran out into the woods and grabbed some fallen branches for a fire, dried moss for tinder, and several rocks to place around the outside of my makeshift campfire. I ran back to my pack and rifled through, grabbing my fire-starting kit. It only took moments for the fire to light as the sparks from the magnesium strip caught.

As the sun set behind the tallest mountain to the west, I warmed myself by the fire, my clothes placed on the ground across from me.

I sat on a mossy log, staring into the flames for what felt like hours, though I couldn't be sure how much time had passed once the sun had gone to rest behind the mountain. Be it shock or the need for warmth, I didn't move, though I knew I had to make preparations for the night.

Finally, I stood up and walked a short distance away to get more wood for the dwindling fire. Once it reignited, I went to my pack, still utterly confused about it being dry and placed against the tree yards away from where I had settled after being carried down the river. I reached for my tent and placed it on a flat grassy patch not far from the flame. I had never been great at setting a tent up and doing it in the darkness made it that much more difficult, yet after some time, I had done it. A sense of accomplishment for the first time since summiting the mountain, what felt like days ago, washed over me.

I sat by the fire a bit longer, all the sounds of the forest drowned out by the rushing water behind me, and tried to make a plan for getting out of the woods in the morning. The trouble was, I realized, I had no idea how far down the river I had been washed. Exhaustion threatened to take me once more, and I determined there was no use making a plan until I had a better idea of my circumstances in the morning. I grabbed my sleeping bag and climbed into my tent, cozy in the confined safety it offered me.

Warm and dry, I closed my eyes, and before long, I was in a deep sleep.

"Alright, everyone, make sure your essays are in by eleven-fifty-nine tonight, or it's a zero. Don't make me the bad guy."

"Hey, Mr. Burke," a tall, blond boy with hair past his shoulders said as he approached me.

"Please, call me Matt," I said for the third or fourth time that day.

He looked at me as if trying to comprehend calling a teacher by his first name but continued, "I know you're new here and all, but I was wondering, could I possibly get an extension on this essay? I've got a lot going on at home, and I have to work tonight, and—"

I held up my hand, stopping him in the middle of his excuse. "Tell you what, I appreciate you coming over and talking to me. Communication is always important. It's Friday night. Why don't we say you get it in to me by Sunday night? Is that fair?"

The student's smile was infectious and genuine. "Yes, absolutely. Thank you so much, I really appreciate it."

"You're very welcome. But this can't be an all-the-time thing, okay?"

"Promise, thanks again, Mr. Burke." He paused as he headed for the door and turned, "Matt."

I smiled and walked back to my desk, happy that my first week was finally complete. I stared out the window and watched as the school buses filled up and the cars shuttled students away from the school. Laughter and talk of the weekend ahead echoed throughout the halls and into the parking lot. I remember thinking that it wasn't that long ago that I was one of those kids, but it could have been a lifetime ago.

I heard the door open to my room, a student asking for another extension, I was sure. I turned around and saw another teacher standing in the doorway. She was beautiful. Brown hair cascaded over her shoulders, glasses framed her crystal blue eyes. Her white blouse flowed as she walked toward me, hand extended. Her smile genuine and true. She was a paragon of beauty.

"Mr. Burke?" she said as I rose from my seat. "I'm Jane Harris. I teach math down the hall. Room 302."

I took her hand in mine. Her skin was soft as flower petals after a summer rain storm. She smelled like summer dew in a field of roses. My heart raced.

"Jane, great to meet you. I'm Matt," I said as I felt my cheeks flushing.

"This is only your first week, right? How have you liked it?"

"Oh, it has been great. Honestly, I've got no complaints, which, working in a school, is a rarity, indeed." We both laughed at this, and I felt on top of the world hearing her genuine joy.

"Are you from around here?"

"Actually, I only just moved here a few weeks ago. I'm still getting to know the area. I mean, you know, I've been up to New Hampshire hiking plenty of times. But getting to know the local hangouts, the best grocery store, and restaurants. That stuff takes some time."

She smiled and looked away for only a moment. She looked at the clock. "Oh, I had better get back to my class and get my stuff packed up. It was great to meet you. I wish we had a bit more time to talk."

As she made her way to the door, I heard my voice speak, though my brain had no idea what was happening. "Well, I do know this one place nearby that has got some great food. Maybe not the best in town, but I was wondering if you'd like to grab something. Maybe you can tell me more about the area? How my taste in food is?"

No sooner had the words left my mouth than utter dread took over. I had never done anything like that before. Never so boldly. So suddenly. She turned back to me slowly. "I…I'm sorry," I stammered. "That probably wasn't professional."

She smiled that angelic smile, and her eyes lit up. "I'd love to, Matt. Care to walk me to my room?"

I had no idea how I had gotten so lucky, but I thought the best course of action was to play this out. Don't question when the universe is working for you.

"I'd love to."

Chapter 7

My eyes snapped open to the cracking of twigs not far from where my head lay. The sun shone through the red lining of the tent, helping my eyes to adjust to the sudden brightness. It felt like I had only just closed my eyes. My heavy eyes threatened to close when I heard what I thought were footsteps again.

I could still hear the roaring of the river nearby, so the breaking branches, I thought, must have been very close to waking me from such a deep sleep. I held my breath and listened intently for any more movement.

I waited for a growl, maybe a roar. Maybe, if I was lucky, a voice calling out to the tent. Though I strained my ears, I could hear nothing but the water lapping the muddy shoreline that I washed up on, the waves crashing over the protruding rocks, the water cascading over the drops in the river. I thought that maybe it was no more than a squirrel or chipmunk having landed its body on the dry wood outside my makeshift camp. *That must be it,* I convinced myself.

I sat up slowly, my back and legs aching from my night on the ground and my float down the mighty Mississippi just outside my tent flap. I actually forced a short laugh at the thought of my body floating gently along the roaring waves of the unnamed river that took me. I rotated my back to one side, and it cracked in several places, loosening the tightness that threatened to hinder me all of the next day. I did the same to the other side and stretched forward as far as I could to touch my toes.

Of course, I was never able to touch my fingers to my toes, even in my youth, but the stretch felt magical this morning.

I unzipped my tent flap, and the sun greeted me, sneaking a peek through the scattering of tree branches that tried their best to conceal it. The smell of pine trees wafted to my nose with the sweet aroma of Christmas. I breathed in deeply and smiled as a wave of nostalgia flooded my mind.

As I crawled out of the tent, my hands landed on the smooth, soft grass. I looked at it, poking its way through the gaps between my fingers, and closed my hands around it. Though the weather had been so cold yesterday, the grass felt as supple as a well-maintained lawn on an early summer morning.

As I stood, I noticed how warm it truly was today. Yesterday's cold morning had given way to the sun's urge to be felt. I looked ahead, finally seeing around me with new eyes. I looked to my left, where the river roared, and the commanding cliff wall stood beyond it. The wall of rock went on as far as my eyes could see. Climbing that would be next to impossible, and that was if I dared to cross the river, which I did not. I had spent long enough in its freezing water and risking being swept further downstream was not anything I wished upon myself.

In front of my tent, the woods were deep and thick. The tree trunks battled for position among the ground; the branches, rising to the heavens, fought their own ancillary battles above. Far above, birds danced among the trees, though their voices were but muted songs drowned out by the river. A gentle breeze made its way through the branches, moving them to the side and allowing the sun to warm my face, a few moments of pure pleasure.

A snap, much louder this time, thundered behind me over the sound of the water. I spun quickly, expecting to fight for my life against some forest beast, yet nothing was there. What I did see, however, was the log I had been sitting on the night before split in two. I wondered how a log thick enough to hold my body weight could simply snap under its own.

"It couldn't," I said as I scanned the area, slowly making my way over to it. My eyes darted back and forth, trying to catch a glimpse of something, anything that could explain how this had happened.

I knelt next to the log and examined it. This log was at least a foot thick. It had to be a bear or a moose that had stumbled upon it. My mind raced with the possibilities, but no bear or moose, or anything else for that matter, could get away so quickly. I stood, hands on my hips, and stared down at the splintered wood.

My eyes drifted past the log to the side opposite where I was standing. There were tracks pushed into the moist ground. Tracks unlike anything I had ever seen before. They weren't exactly human, but humanlike. There were four extremities that I could only imagine were toes, though I thought they were too long and thin to be. What I thought would be the foot itself was wide at the heel, thin in the middle, and wide once more where the toe-like extremities protruded.

If this was a human track, it was unlike any I had ever seen. *Furthermore,* I thought, *why wouldn't they have said something to get my attention? Why would they be out here in bare feet? And where the hell could they have gone?*

A chill ran down my spine. Something strange was in these woods, and I needed to find my way out. Just then, several yards in front of me, dirt kicked up, and a log that was lying across the ground held in place on one side by the trunk of the tree it had fallen from and the other side between two rocks that it had fallen perfectly between, bounced up and down, as though someone or some*thing* had just run over it.

My mouth hung agape, and I froze in place, watching for any more movement. After several seconds, I realized I must have been hallucinating. A strong breeze must have simply blown through the area. I had been looking directly at the log when it moved; there was simply nothing there to have moved it.

I took a deep breath to calm myself.

As I turned back to my camp and looked around, I saw dense woods, too thick to make any real progress on two sides and the thunderous river on the third. I turned back to the log that looked to still be trembling and understood that was the only way to go. My only option was laid out clearly in front of me.

I scratched the back of my head and said to the trees, "It was nothing. Nothing's there." But as I stepped over the strange footprints and the broken log that I had used as my bench, somewhere in the back of my mind, a soft voice whispered what I knew to be true.

You're not alone out here. You need to find your way home. Now.

I began to disassemble my tent and pack my bag.

The woods awaited me.

The sun was high above me when I finally sat down, my back pressed against a pine tree that rose majestically into the sky.

I rifled through my pack, looking for the granola bars that I had packed, maybe some trail mix, and coming across an orange that had somehow managed to not be crushed in yesterday's escapade. The warmth of the sun was soothing against my skin, the complete antithesis of how I had felt coming out of the river.

As my fingernail pierced the skin of the orange, I was overwhelmed by the sweet smell of the fruit. My mouth immediately began to water, and the growl my stomach made was only comparable to the roar of a grizzly. I realized at that moment that I was really in trouble. I had walked for hours in the only direction I could reasonably go, and I was no closer to finding a way out than when I had started. I wasn't so worried about water. I had plenty of filtration if I needed to drink from the river or, in a pinch, a puddle. But food was going to be an issue. I was already low when I came down off the summit of Mount Whitehorse. If I spent too much longer amongst the trees, I would find dire circumstances, indeed.

I savored the orange slice as its juices coated my tongue. Never in my wildest dreams could I have imagined a fruit to taste so good. I decided after several slices, feeling rejuvenated, that I would save the rest for later. I needed to be careful, cautious to the fullest extent. I placed the orange carefully back into my pack and stood up from my seat among the pine needles and cones.

As I continued, my eyes searched the trees and the sky for any sign of a way out. Any path that was more well established. There was nothing but woods too thick to travel safely or with any semblance of haste. I came to a rise on my trail, not anything close to the elevation gain I saw on the Alpine Staircase, but far steeper than I cared to attempt with only half an orange worth of energy in my belly.

"This is crazy," I said as I sucked air into my lungs, now burning with exhaustion.

I ran my fingers through my hair and thought about what to do. I had no plan at this point, nothing more than a vague idea of where I was going. The sun was already on its way to the horizon, and I needed a plan.

A grunt emanated from behind me, soft enough that I had to initially question if it was there. A second grunt confirmed my fear before I even had time to turn around. When I turned and saw a baby moose, rust-colored and tall, my blood ran cold.

Where there is a baby, Mama is always close by, my father had told me. *Do not get caught near her calf.*

The young moose was no more than a dozen yards away from me when I began hearing branches cracking and leaves crunching under something massive. When the giant brown head appeared from between the trees, adrenaline immediately kicked in. The cow turned her head toward me, and I turned just as quickly and ran up the rise.

I instantly knew the error of my ways when I heard the cow utter a short, deep bark and the thunderous hooves quickly running behind me. I hadn't even made it halfway up the rise when I knew I would be caught and trampled by this massive creature, crushed under the weight of its hooves and the fury of a mother protecting her young.

I once again acknowledged that I would soon know what it felt like to die.

I could feel the cow's breath on my back as I struggled up the incline. However, at the last moment, my instinct for survival took over, and I turned sharply, darting into the thick forest. The massive body of the moose ran straight through where I had just been, head down and eyes wild. It tried to stop its forward momentum abruptly and stumbled to the ground, its great body landing hard and rolling forward.

I took a moment to catch my breath, clawing for every ounce of energy I could muster, knowing I was not safe yet. My head snapped around, searching for a way to escape. Nothing but thicket greeted me. As I looked back at the cow, I saw that she was rising to her full height once more, and her eyes were searching for me. My heart began to race as I knew there was no way to get past her.

Crunching behind me made my heart sink to depths I can not describe. I slowly turned as the moose sniffed the air, searching for my scent. Behind me, a tramped-down path began to appear before my eyes. Bushes were flattened, and in some places, the trees appeared to suck in their trunks, allowing for safe passage.

The call that came from the cow's throat startled me by its closeness. A bellow from a larger animal responded somewhere in the distance. The cow had seen me. We locked eyes, and once again, I ran.

I ran with every bit of energy and adrenaline that my body could spare. The path continued to clear before me somehow as I chanced a look over my shoulder. I couldn't rationalize what I was seeing. The forest was closing in on itself again. Where I had just been, thick bushes and trees hampered the way of the cow moose. She fought to get through the dense brush, but the branches scratched at her and poked at her skin and eyes. She stopped only feet into the forest. I continued to run.

With my heart pounding in my head and the crunching of the forest floor beneath my feet, I did not hear the enormous bull moose running directly toward me from my side. Just before it struck me, its bellow made me aware of its presence. His head lowered. It struck me with the force of a train. I flew through the air and landed in a heap on the ground. Stunned and in utter painful misery, I forced myself to look up at the magnificent being that stood before me. It brought its muzzle down only inches from my face. I smelled its stink as it breathed in mine. The fur tickled my face, a tender caress from a powerful force.

My eyes closed, and my brain swam. I had no idea if I would wake up again, and, at that moment, I didn't care either way. A calmness had taken over my body.

As my consciousness faded I was aware of soft whispering just beyond my head. I forced my eyes open, tears corrupting my view. The blurry, brown body of the moose still stood over me, yet a tall figure stood next to it. The figure's skin appeared to be green with flowing brown hair. It appeared to be human, with the strong body of a naked male, yet no genitalia that I could make out. From my blurry eyes, the humanlike being seemed to be speaking to the massive animal. I moved my hand as if to reach out and ask for help.

The being looked down at my crumpled body. A gasp came from its strange mouth, and both he and the moose darted off in opposite directions.

I lost my fight with consciousness and drifted away.

Chapter 8

Some time had passed since the day I had first laid eyes on Jane. Our courtship was magical, full of laughter and passion. Our nights felt endless because we never wanted to sleep, afraid of losing even a moment with each other. Those days were some of the happiest of my life. So when she told me over dinner one night that she was pregnant, I was elated.

Jane cried and told me she was worried about what my reaction would be. She said she was afraid because the baby wasn't planned. That because we had tried to be careful, I'd think she got pregnant on purpose.

I had never seen this part of her before. I wrapped her up in my arms that night and told her that I couldn't be happier. I told her we would be great parents. I told her I couldn't have asked for better news.

In truth, of course, I was nervous. But my nerves were calmed by the absolute certainty that this was meant to be. I was sure that this child would be destined for something great, something important. I guess all parents feel that way about their children.

Jane wiped away her tears and smiled. She kissed my lips tenderly and thanked me. I told her there was no need to thank me for feeling this way and pulled her tighter to me once more. I realized then that I had made the mistake of assuming she was as happy as I was. My heart sank, and I stammered as the words came haphazardly out of my mouth. "Jane, are you happy?"

She pulled her head away from my chest and stared at me with narrowed eyes, seemingly unsure if I was genuinely asking. Realizing my sincerity, she slapped me playfully on the chest and said that, of course, she was.

Relief washed over me as I kissed her lips. I lifted her up from her chair and wrapped my arms around her, lifting her up into my arms. As the flames of passion ignited, I carried her to the couch and laid her down gently. She wrapped her legs around my hips as our tongues danced with each other.

Even after months together, I still had no idea how I had gotten so lucky.

It was a Thursday morning, sunny and warm, four months after our night of lovemaking on the couch. Four months after the happiest day of my life.

Jane and I were sitting on the deck, jotting names down in a notebook, enjoying the breakfast I had gotten up early to cook, her favorite—homemade French toast, scrambled eggs, and a giant glass of chocolate milk—when I noticed a small red stain pooling underneath her as she shifted in her seat. My heart skipped, and no sooner had I asked her to look, a sharp pain in her stomach bent her forward, her chin almost touching her knees.

I helped her to stand and brought her to the car as quickly as possible, terrified at what might be happening and agonizing over the fact that there was nothing I could do. To Jane's credit, she remained as calm and as collected as she could during something so stressful. I held her hand as I drove, and she focused on taking slow, deep breaths. Several times, I heard her breath catch in her throat, and I knew the stabbing feeling she had described was intensifying.

By the time we got to the hospital, blood had soaked through her pants and onto the passenger seat. I ran to get a wheelchair and call for help; a nurse standing by the registration desk followed me to my car and brought her straight into the examination room. I felt completely useless, standing there at her shoulder. I could say nothing. I could do nothing but simply be there.

The doctor took her away for some testing. I walked next to her, the emotional rollercoaster I was riding stuck on the lowest part of the track. She spoke no words but looked up at me with fear in her eyes. She was outwardly strong, but I saw into her soul through her eyes. My heart was wrenching.

When the doctor met us in Jane's room a while later, his tone was grave. He told us that we had lost the baby. She finally allowed herself to cry as she pressed her head into my shoulder.

I placed my head on hers, and our tears carried the monumental weight of abject misery down our cheeks.

Chapter 9

My head throbbed deeply, rhythmically, as I lay in the dirt, unable to open my eyes and face the sun's blazing rays. My ribs felt shattered, further intensifying my will to pass from this world. I hazarded moving a leg carefully, slowly. I rotated my right foot, cautiously testing my pain tolerance, flexing my toes to make sure they still worked. Finding the pain not too intense, I bent my right leg at the knee and set it flat on the ground. Once more, the pain ebbed with the movement.

A slight twisting of my back sent a shockwave of hot pain through my core. I was convinced my back was broken, and I clenched my eyes further shut against the emotional pain that threatened to overwhelm the physical. However, as I lay there, unsure of how I would ever leave these woods, I realized the pain was centered in only one small portion of my back. The throbbing of my head clouded my perception, but as

I concentrated, I could feel the sharp poking of a root, or maybe a rock, threatening to pierce my skin.

I placed my other foot on the ground and used the minute strength I had to slowly roll myself off the sharp object that had given me such fear. When I was on all fours, my head only inches from the dirt and roots that I had laid among for an unknown amount of time, I finally willed my eyes open. I blinked away the tears and dirt that muddied my vision and saw the flattened, smooth area where I had lain. In the middle, a sharp root poked out slightly from the ground, the tip of which was red with drying blood. I groaned and raised myself up to a kneeling position, running a full body check within my mind, scanning myself mentally for injuries. I lurched forward as a searing pain tore through me, centering on my stomach. I lurched over at my knees.

"You're hurt," came a soft, innocent voice from behind me.

My heart skipped so hard that I thought it would cease to start again. I turned around and backed quickly against the tree whose root had stuck me. My breath was rapid, my eyes not wanting to make the connection to my brain, admitting what was in front of me.

A young girl, no more than eight or nine years old, was squatting down only a few feet in front of my seated position against the tree. Her purple shirt was dirty but not tattered. Her brown pants had the look of a comfortable pair that had seen the wear of time. Her face wore a knowing smile that was far beyond her years.

Her brown hair hung past her shoulders and carried with it leaves of varying colors. I couldn't help but think that the leaves looked placed, decorating her. I couldn't imagine how she was here. Why? I had seen no sign of anyone since arriving at the trailhead yesterday morning. Suddenly, a young girl appears. It made no sense.

"H-how? How are you here?" And then suddenly, it occurred to me. I stood faster than I should have, and the jolt of pain from my stomach stunned me into place. "Where's your mom and Dad? I'm lost. I've been lost since yesterday. I fell into the river, and it carried me downstream."

The little girl raised herself up and simply stared at me with a smile that grew too wide for her face. She was silent and let me continue.

"Please, where are your parents? I need help."

She stepped closer to me and took my hand without a word. I let her guide me past the gnarled ground and to a flatter area, where she released my hand and stepped closer to a precipice that seemed to appear from nowhere. She stood silently as the light wind blew through her hair. Loose strands crossed over her face, yet the leaves stayed where they were placed.

Slowly, very slowly, I approached the edge. The trauma of having fallen only yesterday clung to me like the sopping shirt I had on when I crawled out of the river. The drop seemed impossible. We had to be hundreds of feet up, yet I had descended most of the way down the Alpine Staircase and was carried even further down the river. I gasped as the wind pushed me closer to the edge; I forced myself back against the blowing, giving myself a few more feet of distance from the drop that would surely mean death.

The girl stood silently.

"I think it's time to go find your parents. And I don't think they'd want you so close to the edge. Why don't you take a step back, huh?"

She spoke softly, barely audible over the light breeze, "My parents aren't here."

I stepped closer, unsure if I had heard her correctly. "Your parents aren't here?"

The girl shook her head and continued to stare off into the distance, seemingly unbothered by the void that lay only a few feet in front of her. I followed her eyes to the horizon but couldn't make out what she was looking at. A hawk flew overhead, its body contrasting vividly against the blue sky. For the first time in minutes, her head moved as her eyes followed the bird.

"Where are your parents?" I asked when her head lowered once more.

"I don't know. I don't remember them. I only remember this place. I've been here for so long."

Her words made no sense to me. Surely, she had a home. She must have loving parents who were worried about her; they were likely right on the trail that was certainly just out of eyesight. But I couldn't understand why I couldn't hear them calling to her.

"Come on," I said as enthusiastically as I could. "Let's get back to the trail. I'm sure we'll find them. They've got to be close by."

The girl turned and looked at me, her gaze piercing into my soul. "There is no trail. I know this place, these woods. There is only one way out, and it is a long journey."

I had no idea what she was talking about, but if she knew a way out of there, I was willing to follow her. I was sure she would bring us to a parking lot where her mother and father would be waiting for her. They would see her, and their worry would be replaced by elation. They'd run to her and embrace her, and she'd hug them back and apologize for running off without them. They'd kiss her and tell her they loved her and to never do anything like this ever again.

Then worry would take over again as they looked past their daughter to see me. A strange man who had been walking with their baby for untold hours. What had I done to her? They'd approach me cautiously, and her father would ask me who I was and how I came about their daughter. Her mother would politely thank me for bringing her back to them, but she'd grasp her daughter close to her body, still unsure of my part in her disappearance and return.

I'd tell them about my fall and getting lost in the woods. I'd explain to them that their daughter was, in fact, my hero for guiding me back to civilization. That they should be proud of her because, without her, I'd still be wandering in the woods, likely counting down the minutes before I would inevitably die of hunger, exposure, or animal attack.

I thought all this while she turned back to the precipice and pointed off into the distance. "We have to go over there."

I followed her finger to a large rock wall seemingly miles away. "There?" I asked as I pointed as well. "The rocks way over there?"

The girl nodded and lowered her hand.

"That's impossible. How could you have walked that far by yourself? That must be a day or more walk from here."

"Three days." She nodded and turned away from me, walking back in the direction that we had come from. "I told you," she said as she passed, "I've been here a long time."

As I watched her casually step over roots and rocks alike, I found myself thinking of the stories I had heard of children raised by wolves or other animals after becoming lost in the woods. I always thought those stories to be made-up tales of morality, something that parents would tell their children to make sure they were always safe. But the way this child walked through the thicket seemed so natural. I shook my head to clear my thoughts. The only thing that mattered was that she said she knew how to get out.

I realized then that my body felt fine. Somehow, I had only the dullest ache in my stomach and nothing more. I had escaped serious injury and certain death.

I followed her with my gaze and knew what I would do. I would make sure she was safe until I could get her home, back to her parents. Then I would go back to my family and hold them the way that I imagined her family would hold her when they saw her again. My heart swelled by the thought of holding them close.

I took a few steps in the direction that she was walking and said, "I'm Matt. What's your name?"

She stopped mid-stride and turned her head toward me. "I don't remember," she said and continued to walk past the flattened dirt patch that had once held my crumpled body.

Chapter 10

It was several weeks past Christmas, and the snow pelted the window with unending flakes that caked themselves onto the screen. A full moon rose above but was blocked out by the clouds that were releasing the torrent of frozen precipitation on the city of Boston. It was one-fifteen a.m. and Jane lay in the hospital bed with her legs held by a nurse and myself, pushing our daughter into this strange world.

Two years had passed since that terrible day in the doctor's office. Jane had been depressed for weeks after the news, and I laid in bed right next to her on those quiet nights. We spoke little to each other, both of us so fragile we thought that any noise could break the weak shell we had cast around ourselves, protecting our emotions—our sanity.

During those few weeks, words were not needed. We both felt the loss, and we both processed it in our own ways. We needed each other. We just couldn't put the need into words. Touch became our communication. When emotion threatened to overtake me, I would reach out and intertwine my fingers with hers. When tears flowed from her eyes, and she silently wept, she'd put her head on my shoulder until my shirt was soaked through.

Sometimes, words can get in the way.

Sometimes, you just need to be present.

Jane pressed down hard and pushed. I pushed her leg toward her chest slightly as my hand lay in hers, my fingers white from the crushing strength of her primal nature.

"You're doing great, honey," I said to her in between her screams. She looked me in the eyes, and I could see several emotions pass over her face simultaneously. The most obvious being a strange dichotomy of love and hate. I smiled at her, hoping to ease her pain somehow.

"One more push should do it," the doctor said as she looked between my wife's legs, guiding our daughter's head forward. Easing her into the cold air that would soon shock her system.

Jane's screams silenced, and her face turned a shade of red that masqueraded as purple. I turned toward my daughter's head just in time to see a gush of fluid and a grayish body explode into the world. Jane released her breath in a heavy sigh as her head fell back onto the pillow. Her head snapped up only seconds later as panic flooded her. "Why isn't she crying? Matt, why isn't she crying? What's going on?"

I had followed one of the nurses to the scale on the other side of the room and watched our daughter blink twice while staring at me, Jane's words lost somewhere in time. Her black hair was matted down on her little head, which was shaped a bit like an ice cream cone. The nurse wiped the vernix off her body, and still, she remained quiet.

"Matt!" Jane called loudly, snapping me back to the time and place where my body stood.

At the sound of her raised voice, our baby began to cry. As the doctor worked between my wife's legs, she put her hand to her mouth and closed her eyes, completely unable to stop the tears of joy that overflowed. As they brought our baby over, wrapped in a warm towel that engulfed all but her face, Jane reached her arms above herself. They placed the baby on her chest, and our daughter immediately stopped crying as she looked into her mother's eyes.

"Hi," Jane cooed, her smile so wide I thought it might tear her face.

"Do you have a name picked out?" asked the nurse who stood over mom and child, her aged face showing that no matter how many times she witnessed this tender moment, it would never get tiring.

"Laura," Jane said, not taking her eyes off our daughter's.

I remember feeling as though a snapshot was taken at that moment. My eyes blinked, creating the effect of a shutter closing and capturing this magical moment in posterity. I walked to the top of the bed and kissed Jane on the forehead, then I leaned down to tenderly kiss Laura's head. I remember the way she smelled. Even to this day, I can recall the smell of her with only a moment's thought.

As I stepped back and looked at my girls, I realized how lucky I truly was. Pride swelled within me, but simultaneously, fear did as well. The world was a dangerous place, especially for women. Kidnappers, murderers, rapists, they all passed by my mind's eye in a march of madness. I had no idea how I would protect them, but I knew I would have to. I knew someday I'd need to.

In that moment, my father's face flashed before me, and a renewed sense of confidence overtook me. I remembered the day on those ladders, and my mind was at ease.

A few days passed, and the hospital discharged Jane and Laura. I had spent the last couple of days making sure the baby seat was in the car correctly and that we had enough food, baby wipes, and diapers to get us through at least the first week at home.

As the hospital attendant wheeled the two through the automatic doors, my heart once more began to race. I knew we were as prepared as we could be, but that nagging question, "What if?" attacked my thoughts.

I put baby Laura into her car seat and helped Jane into the passenger seat before heading home. I kept the car five miles below the speed limit and let Jane take care of most of the conversation as I white-knuckle focused on the task at hand.

When we pulled into the driveway, I unbuckled Laura from her seat as Jane made her way slowly to the front steps. I had gotten used to carrying our newborn child so light in my arms I was afraid she'd blow away in the breeze, but it didn't stop my heart from racing and thinking about all the things I could do wrong.

Jane let herself into our home and left the door open for us as she gingerly made her way to the couch. I stopped on the top step and kissed Laura once more. Her eyes flickered from side to side but remained closed. Her lips opened and closed as though she was trying to feed; her movements brought such joy to me.

That joy only lasted for a few moments, however. The smell of fast food, cheeseburgers to be exact, washed over me, followed at once by a sense of dread that was so profound I thought I would fall over right there with Laura in my arms. No sooner did the startling feeling wash over me before it was gone. The phantom smell wafted away into the ether as well. When I looked back to Laura, her eyes were open, staring at me.

"Come on, baby, let's go find Mom."

Chapter 11

I watched the young girl, walking several feet ahead of me, as she glided with ease through the dense thicket that felt, to me, alien. She spoke very little, and she seemed to lose very little energy even after hours of walking in a direction that felt opposite to where she had been pointing earlier.

"Are you sure we're going the right way?" I asked for what must have been the fourth time in as many hours.

She did not even turn her head in my direction but instead just raised a thumb on her little hand and skipped forward at a quicker pace. I sighed and slowed my pace in an attempt to catch my breath. "Hey, hang on just a second. I'm exhausted," I managed to wheeze out between inhalations. As I leaned down and pressed my hands against my knees, I realized the utter silence that had overtaken the forest.

The buzzing of silence in my ears broke when I heard the sound of cracking branches behind me. I envisioned the moose returning, having followed me all day, waiting for a chance to strike and finish the job of stomping my weakened body into the earth. I turned once more to the place where the girl had been walking and realized she was not there.

"Hey…hey girl. You need to come back here. It's not safe." I took a few steps in the direction we had been going when I heard more branches snapping, closer this time. When I turned back, I saw a shadow moving in the tangle of the forest. Though I couldn't get a clear image of it, I thought it was walking on two legs, dancing between the trees. And, were those…wings?

I yelled loudly in the direction of whatever was watching me. I raised my hands over my head and yelled louder, even chancing a step forward in an attempt to scare the thing off. When next I heard the footsteps they sounded as though they were heading in the opposite direction, and with some speed. I stood stock-still with my arms raised until my fingers began to tingle. I realized how stupid I must have looked and lowered my arms, embarrassed. I laughed at myself and shook my hands vigorously, trying to get the feeling back in my fingers.

The sun was beginning to fall below the treeline, and I began to wonder where we'd set up camp for the night. Gray clouds were rolling in from the west, and the air had an electric charge to it, a sure sign of a storm rolling in. As if on cue, the wind cut through the trees and sent a chill down my spine. My heart leaped into my throat as I realized the little girl had disappeared minutes ago and did not respond to my calls before I scared the thing in the thicket off.

"Shit, shit, shit," I said, panicking as I dashed forward. "Hey, little girl, where are you? Can you hear me?" I shouted into the forest. I stood and listened, but no response came back. My eyes were frantic, searching for any sign of her. Listening for her calling back from a distance. If only the damned wind would stop blowing. I was sure that whatever animal I had scared away was surely stalking her now. My breathing became rapid, and I let loose one more yell in the direction in which I was sure she had gone.

The wind stopped.

"Why are you yelling?"

I whipped my head back around, and there she was, standing just behind me, holding out several white mushrooms. Her eyes were confused, but her smile showed that she found my panic amusing.

"Where have you been? I've been calling you. You can't just disappear on me. We're in this together. We need to find our way out."

Her eyes changed to match her smile, and she thrust her arm out, urging me to take the mushrooms. "Go on, you need to eat."

I looked down at them and took a step back. "No way. You can't just go eating mushrooms you find in the forest. Are you crazy? I don't want to be stumbling around hallucinating or, worse, hunched over in pain because I ate some—"

"You'll be fine," she said as she pushed them against my chest and stepped back. "I know these woods."

I looked down, and my stomach growled in response. I was about to urge caution once more when I saw her reach into her own pockets and grab one of the white fungus herself, immediately putting it into her mouth. I reasoned that in order for her to survive, she must have learned what to eat and what not to. Maybe she wasn't so much lost out here but instead was the child of some hermit who made his life living off the grid. I decided to take a chance and sample a small bite.

"Hey, this is pretty good."

"I thought you'd like them."

As I savored the sweet, earthy taste, I realized that she was staring in the direction of the thing that I had scared away. When I stepped closer, I saw her eyes scanning the path and the woods just surrounding it. It was as though she was sensing something that wasn't seen.

"Hey, you okay?" I didn't want to bring up what I had scared off. I thought it might make her panic, and a scared child, especially one that seemed to be my only way of escape from these woods, was not something I wanted.

Her eyes met mine. I felt like I could see eternity within them. She was young but seemed so knowledgeable. Just behind her gaze was a sense of caution and something else. I thought it was fear, but I shook it off, her confidence winning me over with every passing moment. She looked past me and to the sky, seeming to notice suddenly the sun having difficulty fighting its way through the trees. The red of her shirt…

"Wait," I said with sudden concern, "when did you get that sh—"

"Come on, we need to find a safe place to sleep for the night. We can't stay here."

She marched past me in the direction that we had been walking, her pace quickening with each step. I looked over my shoulder at the darkening shadows that were encroaching upon me and moved quickly to catch up.

"Through here," she said without turning around. She pushed down the branches that blocked our path. Each small step shrouded her deeper in shadow.

"Hey, where are we going? It's getting dark."

Silence.

"Hey. Hey, come back."

Silence. Then, "Will you come on?"

With a sigh and one last glance over my shoulder, I pushed the branches down and stepped further into the darkness. My vision tried to adjust to the darkened woods as I walked, guided only by the silhouetted view of the young girl ducking deftly under the outstretched limbs. I stumbled over roots, and my ankle turned on a rock that was covered by dampened leaves. I grunted and begged her to slow down.

"Keep straight," she shouted back. "We're almost there."

"Almost where?"

Silence.

As my frustration rose, I pushed hard against the branches, tugging at my hair. I spun around when the sound of cushioned footsteps behind me sounded. Darkness had inundated the area from whence I came. The fear of being lost in the woods with night rapidly approaching and no fire for warmth or security chilled me to my core. I didn't even realize that I had been walking backward when something grabbed my arm. I spun around once more, fight or flight instincts ready to kick in.

"We're here."

The forest opened up into a field that seemed out of place among the thick trees that ringed it. The moon was rising now, but the darkness away from the trees wasn't absolute. The grass was lush, and after walking for so long over roots and rocks, the feeling of stepping onto the soft ground was wonderful. The serenity of this area was like nothing I had ever experienced. It was like sitting by a warm fire while the snow raged outside. It offered comfort amid fear.

"What is this place?" I asked the girl, awestruck by the feeling that had overtaken me.

"It's safe here. Nothing will bother us."

I looked down at her and wondered at the truth of that statement. Was she just trying to make me feel better? Make me feel safe? I was the adult here, and I felt like I was failing her.

She walked a few steps away from me and held out a finger. She began to giggle, a sound unlike any that I had heard from her yet. A sound of happiness. A child's sound.

"Look," she said joyfully. "They are everywhere here. This is how you know we're safe."

I walked to her side and saw a large dragonfly sitting on her outstretched finger. The being's blue body was reflecting the moonlight into the girl's eyes, giving them a slight glow that had not been there previously. Her smile spread so wide I thought her cheeks might tear open, and suddenly, she reminded me of Laura. The joy that comes from the simple pleasures in life. The giggles and laughter that can fill your heart to the point of bursting. The wonder in a child's eyes as they discover the beauty in all the world's chaos.

The dragonfly's wings began to flap at an unimaginable speed, and the girl lifted her hand toward the sky as it flew off. She watched it as it disappeared into the moonlight, and a sigh escaped her lips. Suddenly, there were dozens of dragonflies darting in between our bodies. Reds, blues, and yellows created a moving rainbow that danced among us. I held my hand out in joyous wonder and had several immediately land on it.

"See," she said, "they will protect us."

I had no idea what she meant, but I knew the feeling that had overtaken me. There was something special about this place. I couldn't explain it, but I knew, for at least this night, we were safe.

As I set up the tent, the girl danced with the dragonflies a few yards away. Once the tent was upright, I began working on the fire while the girl rummaged through my bag, looking for any remaining food that I might have. She pulled out a can of Spaghettios and tossed it in my direction as I warmed my hands by the fire.

"Where did you get this?" I said, curiosity and caution in my voice.

"In your bag, silly. You don't remember what you packed?"

I knew I hadn't packed this. I hadn't even had Spaghettios since I was a kid, but they were Laura's favorite. Maybe she had stuck it in my pack before I left. Maybe?

This place was esoteric. It almost seemed magical.

It had been a long day so I decided to not question what was happening. We were hungry, and we needed sleep. We warmed the can near the flame and pulled out a spork that I always carried with me (a necessity for my pack with or without canned food), and we ate in silence.

When I climbed into the tent, the girl stood outside looking in.

"If you'd rather, I could sleep outside, and you can have the tent," I said, feeling foolish at my lack of awareness of the situation. Of course she wouldn't want to sleep next to me. She's not Laura.

She shook her head no and climbed in quietly.

She curled up into a ball next to me and was snoring before the tent was zipped up.

Chapter 12

The man who walked past Laura the Friday before her birthday was nondescript in every way but one. He was of average height and average build. His hair was covered under a wool winter hat, one of the ones with a puff ball on the top that flopped around as you walked. His eyes were cast down so as to not give his thoughts away. His left hand was tucked into his jeans pocket. The only distinctive feature on this man was a set of letters, one on each finger of his right hand—W-R-A-T-H.

The man could have been anyone. In some ways, he was. He was no one, and he was everyone.

That's how he got so close.

I remember Laura looking so happy as she walked by the man. She glanced at me in the Jeep before returning to her conversation with her friends—her teacher walked a few steps behind. It was January fourteenth, and the sky hung low with gray clouds that promised snow later that evening. A snowy evening felt fine to me. It was just another excuse to light the fire and sit in a darkened room full of Christmas lights that I had stubbornly refused to take down.

The fog of their breath rose toward the clouds as they giggled. I waved to her when her eyes caught mine, and she waved back. Her smile showed a child's innocence. She had not a care in the world because she knew if I was there, she was safe. In my heart, I knew that to be true as well, but in my mind, I often questioned how one so averse to risk could protect something as fragile as a child. Children look to their parents for guidance, yes, but children often learn by doing. You can not protect your child from all the pains of the world. You can only hope to raise them to be smart enough to avoid the fiercest of them.

The tattooed man's head moved just slightly in my direction as he walked by, perhaps enough to see my face out of his peripheral vision. Perhaps not.

I leaned over and opened the back door a little as Laura approached with her teacher. Laura was small for her age but smart enough to get herself situated in her booster seat while her teacher and I spoke through the rolled-down passenger seat window.

"Laura had another great day today, Mr. Burke. You should be very proud."

I looked back at her and smiled proudly as she clicked the seatbelt into place. "I am, thank you."

"She's only in first grade. If she keeps this up, she's going to be cruising right through elementary school." Her teacher looked back at Laura, who was watching the interaction keenly, listening to the praise that was being heaped upon her and filling her with a six-year-old's version of pride. Her teacher pressed the back door shut tightly and gave me another warm smile before turning back to the waiting children, ready to be picked up by their parents, anxious to go home to the warmth of pajamas and hot cocoa.

I gave a wave and rolled up the passenger window before edging my way out onto the road. The entire ride home, Laura talked. First, about her day in school and how her teacher had brought in cupcakes for everyone in honor of her upcoming birthday party. Second, about her actual party the next day. She was only turning seven, but Laura took her birthdays very seriously and wanted to ensure everyone would have a great time.

She had insisted on having it at home, which was more than fine in my and Jane's eyes. This idea saved us money renting a place out for the day, and besides, with the current weather forecast, it looked like it was the safest plan. She had the balloons picked out, the cake specially designed with a wolf on it—her favorite animal—and what movie they'd watch after she opened her presents and they got to eat all the wolf cake. I knew how much fun she'd have, and that made me swell with happiness.

By the time we walked in the front door and Jane was greeting me with a soft kiss, the first fat snowflakes began to fall.

The next morning, after all the kids arrived and were busy tearing the living room apart, I sat with Jane at the kitchen table, talking about a family trip to the beach—maybe Florida or South Carolina—sometime in the spring. I was never much of a beach-goer, but the girls were, and I figured a trip was a trip, and I could get plenty of pleasure out of just being away from home for a few days.

The snow had stopped falling overnight, but a fresh coating of fluffy snow danced with the breeze outside the living room windows. The *whooshing* of the wind gave an eerie feeling to an otherwise beautiful afternoon. I remember the girls screaming on one occasion when it blew so hard it rattled the windows, the snow that had been picked up pelting against the glass.

The kids ran over to watch when Laura called out. "Dad, there is a man outside of our house. What's he doing?" Laura's best friend, Sarah, lowered her head and walked back to the toys, alone.

I remember thinking he was probably just some guy out for a walk. It really was a nice day besides the wind. I told her not to worry about it and continued talking about the vacation that would surely be a highlight for the year.

The kids all ran back to play with the toys that were scattered on the ground, all but Laura. She knelt on the couch in front of the window and kept staring outside. I saw her from the kitchen table and thought little of it until she began to wave. When I stood up and made my way next to her, the man had begun his trek down the road once more. His slightly hunched-over walk, hands in the pockets of his long black coat, hood pulled up to conceal his face, gave him the look of a character that belonged in a noir film. The darkness of him was stark against the pristine snowfall of the previous night.

"Come on, Laura. Let's go back and play with your friends. Cake will be out soon."

The word cake seemed to snap her out of a daze, and she gave me a quick kiss on the cheek before taking her place among her dolls and the girls in the furthest corner of the room. I watched her again, my heart swelling once more, wondering at the joy a child can so easily grab ahold of.

That night, when I was tucking Laura snuggly in her bed, I could clearly see that something was bothering her.

"What's wrong, sweetheart?" I asked delicately. Her brow was furrowed, and her eyes lowered as if she was thinking some secret thought that she didn't want to tell.

Laura and I had always had such a close relationship. She was a daddy's girl through and through, so it caught me as very strange that she was so hesitant to tell me what was on her mind. Then again, kids have secrets. We all do. Something tugged at me, and I pressed the issue gently.

"Did you have a fun day?"

She raised her eyes and said, "Oh yes, it was a great day, Dad."

I smiled and sat down next to her. "So why the long face? Something is on your mind."

She lowered her eyes once more and sighed deeply. "Well…"

I put my hand on her back softly. "You can tell me. No matter what, you can always tell me what's bothering you."

She looked up, and her little eyes caught mine. Worry swam in hers, which caused a flash flood of panic in my heart. "Well…that man that was outside today…"

It took me a moment to realize what she was talking about. The stranger had left my mind shortly after he had left my sight. But when your young daughter is concerned about a strange man that had been outside your house, you listen. I edged closer to her. "What about him?"

"I think I know that man."

"Oh really?" I urged further. "From where?"

"He was the man that cleans the trash at my school."

Relief washed over me as I allowed myself to exhale slowly. "Oh, well, that's nice. He must live around here."

Laura shrugged her shoulders and lowered her head once more. "I hope he doesn't live around here," she said softly.

"Why do you hope that, honey? He must be a nice man if he works at your school, right?"

She looked right at me, and with her eyes brimming with tears, she said, "I don't think he's a nice man."

"Why do you say that?"

"I swore I wouldn't tell Sarah's secret."

Memories flashed in my mind of Sarah walking away from the other children as they stared out the window at the man. My concern grew.

Laura and Sarah had met in Kindergarten and immediately bonded. Sarah had already promised Laura that when it was *her* birthday, she wanted to have a sleepover with just the two of them. Laura was very excited about this and was already counting down the days.

My heart sank as dread crept over me. "It's okay, Laura. If Sarah is in trouble, you need to tell someone so that she can be safe. I know you promised, but it's better to be sure your friend is okay."

Laura swallowed deeply and took a deep breath, fighting against the urge to end the conversation abruptly. "That man, he doesn't work at the school anymore. I think it's because of what he did to Sarah."

"What did he do to Sarah?"

Laura sniffed a few times, I think, to choke back the lump that seemed to be in her throat. "Well…she told me that last week she was in the bathroom at school, and she heard the door open. She said the footsteps sounded really heavy, like a big person." She paused here and took another deep breath before continuing. "Sarah said that she saw that man looking through the crack in the door at her while she was peeing."

The weight of that confession hit my heart like a city bus. I couldn't believe that no one from the school had told anyone this. I couldn't believe this guy wasn't in jail. Why was he walking around my neighborhood? Why was he walking around the school? My blood boiled, but I kept a calm facade in front of my daughter.

Tears began to roll down her eyes at this point, and all I could do was tell her it was going to be okay, and that I would go talk to the school on Monday. She knew everything was okay in my arms.

But she wasn't always in my arms.

Chapter 13

A low rumble of thunder sounded somewhere in the depths of my sleeping mind. My eyes flicked back and forth behind closed lids as I fought the urge to fully wake. I could sense that it was the middle of the night, and after a long day of walking, I knew I needed as much sleep as I could get.

Another rumble followed by a quick flash that lit up the tent and made my eyes dart back and forth behind closed lids tugged at my consciousness. Laura's face began to fade from in front of me, and I rolled over roughly, frustrated by the interruption to my rest. When I extended my arm out at my side, something struck me as odd—the girl was gone.

My eyes snapped open, and I sat up in a fever pitch, startled by how quickly I was fully aware of what was around me and what was not.

The pattering of rain falling on the leaves of the trees that ringed the field sounded deafening, and I realized that I could visualize the cascade as it approached me, even while behind a zipped tent flap. When the rain finally fell upon my shelter, I feared what would happen to the girl out in the weather. Exposure was a real concern for me, and my concern was doubly so for her.

Instinctually, I reached for my backpack, knowing that I had a headlamp in the front pocket, before realizing that my pack was near the outside edge of the field. Even a novice camper knows not to sleep with his or her pack in their tent. If a bear comes into camp, it can have dire consequences.

I remembered a story that I had heard on one of the outdoor podcasts that I listened to regularly of a mother and two cubs coming into several tent sites just outside of Yellowstone. The story told of people being woken up in the middle of the night by getting dragged out of their tents, at least one of which was dragged out by his head and brought several yards away. Some lost body parts, another was eaten. The old bear adage of, "*If it's black, fight back. If it's brown, lay down. If it's white, say goodnight*" played over and over in my head when on the trail. I suppose that adage works best when encountering a bear on the trail, not one that is coming into your campsite. The story terrified me but taught me a valuable lesson in regard to where to store your pack overnight.

The thunder clapped much louder this time, and the lightning struck much faster. I knew I had to go outside and find her. We were out in the open, which, while not needing to fear falling trees, left us no shelter, save the nylon green tent that appeared blacker by the minute as the rain crashed upon it.

I unzipped the flap and was immediately greeted by the blowing wind and rain splashing off the grass and into the tent. I crawled out, not bothering with my boots, and began hollering for the young girl.

I was immediately soaked, my hair hanging down and dripping cold water into my eyes as I yelled as loud as I could. It did almost no good as my voice was lost in the howling wind and the claps of thunder that approached at an alarming rate.

I walked further from the tent, further from the relative safety and dryness that had housed me only a short time ago. But I needed to find her. For the better part of a day, she had acted as my protector, my guide through the unknown. How could I allow that to happen? She was just a kid. Whether she lived out here in some hidden cabin or was herself lost, she needed me to be strong so we could find our way back home.

I picked up speed as I hustled toward the darkness of the woods. A clap of thunder, the loudest yet, bombarded me from what sounded like directly above. Immediately, a streak of lightning fizzled through the sky and struck a tree somewhere not too far off into the woods. I could hear the cracking of the wood and the smell of ozone and fire. I screamed for her as loud as I could once more, my voice cracking with the strain.

Then I saw her.

I only saw her for a moment, about a hundred yards ahead of me, during one of the flashes of lightning, but there was no mistaking her slender frame. Her clothes stuck to her body as she stood only a few feet outside of the tree line. She was not alone—at least, I thought she wasn't. It looked like she was talking to something. Something I had thought I had seen before when I had been knocked out by the moose. Something I couldn't explain.

I ran toward her, desperate to get her away from any danger, not worrying about the danger I might be putting myself in. The thunder rumbled loudly overhead, and I knew I would get another clear visual momentarily. When the lightning struck again, my eyes were solely focused on where I had believed the pair to be.

She was, in fact, speaking to someone—something. It was tall. Much taller than myself and towering over her. Its skin was brown, but not like the skin of a native or ethnic person. It almost looked wooden. Its arms seemed to have leaves hanging off of branches that sprung up from the thicker parts. It had no hair, not in the sense of any human hair. Its head seemed to be covered in moss; leaves clung to the ends, intertwined among the stems.

As alien as this being appeared, it did have features familiar to my eyes. It had a mouth, it had dark, sunken eyes, and four limbs. It bent forward, its strange hands pressed against its strange knees. The girl didn't seem to be threatened by it, but I couldn't help but feel uncomfortable with how close it was to her.

By the time the lightning flashed again, I was only about thirty yards away…and it saw me. The tree-like being snapped up straight and began to run back into the relative safety of the forest. However, the girl ran forward and grabbed its arm, turning it back toward her momentarily. I could see her lips moving but could make out no words. The being nodded and ran into the woods just as I was approaching the girl.

I stared off into the distance, my mouth hanging agape. "W-what…what was—"

"You scared them off," she said as though I had startled her old friend and banished them from our home.

"Scared…scared what—"

"Come on," she said as she stomped back toward the tent. "We need to get out of the rain. It's not safe out here."

I was frozen in place for several more seconds, staring off into the depths of the forest, when another thundercrack came and startled me back to reality. The girl was already halfway to the tent. With a glance back over my shoulder, I sprinted to catch up with her, my mind racing as to what I had just seen.

It was time for some answers.

When the girl climbed into the tent I could feel the anger inside myself rising. Not because I was truly mad at her, per se—I was afraid. I had sworn I had seen my father. I had been through a nightmarish time, fighting for survival down a raging river. I had met this strange girl in the woods, alive and somehow thriving when I could barely make my way through the tangle of trees just off any trail. I had been attacked by a moose. I had been stalked by…something else. And I now saw some sort of…being, maybe the one that I was being stalked by—the wings I thought I had seen before it disappeared into the woods haunted my thoughts, though I was hesitant to admit that to myself. My only care was getting us out of this situation, but I was being lied to, and I was going to find out why.

As I climbed into the tent, I cautioned myself about raising my voice. She was still young and somehow my only way out of here. If I scared her away, who knew what would happen to me? Who knew what would happen to her? I sucked in some air between my teeth and sat down next to her, her back already turned as though she were trying to fall asleep.

"I think we need to talk," I said as softly as I could manage.

The girl remained still and silent. Her wet clothes clinging to her little body; she shivered slightly. I wanted to warm her up, but I cautioned against touching her.

"Hey, we really need to talk. You've been hiding things from me."

"I haven't been hiding things. Not on purpose, at least."

I nodded. At least she recognized that she was not telling me things. If we were in this together, I needed her to understand the importance of being completely honest. That's the only way we'd survive. She was obviously much more familiar with these woods and the secrets they held, but she was still a kid. She might not know it, but she needed me as much as I needed her.

"Okay, well, that's a start. I have questions that I need you to answer." The rain pattered lightly on the tent, having slowed some since we entered. "Do you think you can answer them?"

I saw her nod her head slightly, but she remained turned on her side, away from me. I edged back against the far side of the tent, giving her extra room so she did not feel me looming over her, intimidating her.

"Okay, first, how are you here? You're just a kid, but you walk around these woods as though you've been here all your life."

"I have been here all my life. Well, as far back as I can remember, at least."

"But, where are your parents? You said you don't have any parents. That just can't be true. Did you get lost on a hike out here with them or something?"

She paused at this, seeming to be deep in thought before she responded. "I didn't say I don't have parents. I said I don't remember them. It has just been so, so long since I've seen them or heard their voices that I can't remember them well. I can hear my mother's voice faintly if I think really hard, but I can't find her face in my mind." She paused again, and even with her back toward me, I could see her concentrating. "All I can remember is waking up one night in a field."

Trauma works in strange ways. I didn't know if her parents had left her, lost her, or she ran away because she was afraid. But, I could tell, at least at this moment, she was telling me the truth. I knew blocked memories can sometimes work their way back to the forefront of a person's mind. I thought, rather than push the issue, I should ask more, and perhaps, in time, she'd remember and be willing to share.

"Okay, well, how have you survived? I mean, it's not often you find a kid out in the middle of the woods that seems to be thriving, maybe needing a bath…" I smiled when she turned and glared at me with childlike mischief, "But otherwise, doing just fine."

She sat up now, her wet hair still plastered to her scalp. Drops of water reflected by the lightning that still flashed off in the distance fell upon the tent floor. "I guess I just learned."

I looked at her and cocked my head to the side, sensing deception once more. "Listen, if we're going to get through this, we need to be completely honest with each other. I need to trust you, and you need to trust me. It's the only way we're going to make it." I adjusted my position and altered my question, sensing the response to this would give me a better understanding of how she survived. "Is it that thing that I saw you talking to?"

She raised her head to face me. Her eyes were wet, but I couldn't make out if it was from tears or the rainwater that had soaked us. The wind picked up outside again, though the rain continued to slow. Her mouth dropped open as though she were ready to say something and then thought better of it.

I waited.

"That…that's my friend."

My mind swirled. From what I had seen, it was a thing to fear. It was a monster. How could she consider this thing a friend? I didn't even know what that *thing* was, but I knew what I saw. Questions came with rapid fire to my mind, but I slowed them, unwilling to startle the girl with a barrage of potentially invasive questions. I settled on the first one that came into my mind.

"Your friend seemed awfully scary. He didn't look like a person. Not entirely."

The girl curled her knees up to her chest and wrapped her arms around them. "No, he's not a person. But he isn't scary. He's good."

"How do you know he's good?"

"He has always helped me. When I woke up in the field that night, he was there. I remember being scared, too, when I first saw him. I screamed and got up to run. But, he did something strange when he heard me scream."

My curiosity was peaked. "What did he do?"

"He didn't speak. He almost never speaks, even now. But he bent down on a knee and held his hand out. I was scared because, well, you saw. His hands, his arms, don't look like a person's. I wasn't sure what to do, but I took a couple of steps closer. He didn't move. He just kneeled there, waiting for me to feel comfortable.

"When I finally felt brave enough to reach out and touch his hand, he smiled. Well, smiled his kind of smile. I was shocked at how smooth his hands were. I remember thinking, this is a tree. I didn't really know what to expect, but it wasn't the smoothness of his hands. I thought *he must be gentle*. And he always has been."

I couldn't wrap my mind around this. I had seen this being, but listening to this girl talk about it, I thought she must have spent too much time out here, away from society. But…

"And he helped you survive? That's how you've made it so long without your parents?"

The girl nodded. "He's always been there for me." She looked at me once more. "There are others out there. Most of them keep their distance. I've only spoken to one other of his kind, but they're there."

In a daze, I heard my mouth ask without my conscious mind knowing, "What are they?"

"That's hard to explain. I asked him that once before. I told you, he doesn't talk much. He tried to explain, but I couldn't understand. All I got from him was that they are very, very old and have been here since time began."

I couldn't fathom the depths of what she said. It sounded as though these things were…gods. Could that be? Could the stories of lore that I had read when I was a kid be true? Could there really be beings among us that protect the environs that humans toil about in every day? My stomach rolled, and I leaned back against the wall of the tent. I felt the nylon give against my weight and the cold water pour over the outside of the tent and over my back. We sat silent for several minutes before she spoke again.

"There is something else out there, too." Her voice had taken on a tone of ominous fear.

"What's out there?"

She pulled her legs closer to her chest and placed her face against them, hiding her eyes, seeming to not want to look outside of the still-opened tent flap. "Something that really is scary. Sometimes, it follows me."

"What do you mean it follows you? An animal?"

She shook her head vigorously. "No. A monster."

Her breathing picked up, and I felt the need to scooch closer and place my hand on her shoulder, feeling as though she was comfortable enough now to accept my comforting touch. "What do you mean? What does it look like?"

She shook her head hard again, and I could tell that this was not the time to continue with this line of questioning. She began to shiver again as a chill crept deep within me, as well. We had no way to get dry, and with the storm passing, the temperature was dropping minute by minute. I changed the subject.

"Okay, well, we need to get warm, and we're only going to freeze if we keep these soaked clothes on."

She looked at me with a distrustful eye.

"I know how you feel. Frankly, I'm a bit uncomfortable with it myself. But we either do this and stay warm, or we keep them on and risk hypothermia. I don't know about you, but I need to get home to my wife and daughter. And I need to get you to your parents. Can you trust me?"

She thought for a moment and nodded slightly.

"I'll turn my back. You get undressed and climb into the sleeping bag. When you're in, you tell me, and I'll get undressed too." I thought for a moment and added, "I'll keep my underwear on. I'll stay outside the sleeping bag, but we're going to need to huddle together in order to stay warm. Will that be okay?"

The girl's teeth were beginning to chatter, but she was able to shudder out a "yes" in response. I turned my back as she fumbled with her wet clothes, and I could hear her climbing into the warmth of the sleeping bag."

"Okay," she said, "I'm in. Your turn, I'm not looking."

I took off my shirt and pants and immediately felt better without the stickiness of wet fabric pressing against me. She remained turned away from me as I crawled over to the tent flap and grabbed the zipper. As the flap began to close, lightning struck once more, lighting up the treeline. A being stood just outside the field. Not the one that had stood with the girl earlier, but something darker. From my distance and in the short time I had light, I could make out a hulking mass of muscle, red eyes that looked to be embers from a campfire, and a mouth closed in a tight sneer.

My heart skipped, and I almost screamed, but at the last moment, I was unwilling to scare the girl.

As the sky lit up again the being had disappeared, but leaves and branches from the trees high above fell to the ground silently.

Chapter 14

After Laura's breathing became more regular and a small snore escaped her, I laid her head down gently on the pillow. My head swam with disorientation, my heart sank with grief, and my gut raged with fury.

I could hear the TV playing loudly in the living room, one of those mindless housewife stories where the women feigned friendship and exaggerated drama in order to garner television ratings. I could hear Jane laugh at the absurdity of it all, a stark contrast to the dense fog that hung just down the hall.

I got up slowly, careful not to wake Laura from her rest, and made my way on light, determined footsteps down the hall.

"Honey, you should see what this woman just did." Jane's face instantly changed when she saw the pallor of my own. She reached for the remote as I stood next to the couch. The volume lowered, and she told me to sit.

I sat frozen, Jane equally so as she waited for me to tell her what had happened. I rubbed my hands across my face, trying to snap myself out of the stupor that I found myself in. Jane edged closer to me and put her hand on my knee, a caring gesture.

"Did you have any idea what was going on at Laura's school?"

Jane shook her head. "No, what do you mean?"

I turned to face my wife, her eyes now filled with worry. "Laura just told me something very disturbing. Apparently, one of the janitors…he was let go for peeping on the girls in the bathroom. Sarah, specifically."

Jane gasped and brought her hand to her mouth. She sat back on the couch, and her eyes flicked back and forth, trying to make sense of the information.

"But Sarah was just here. She didn't seem out of sorts. Why haven't we heard anything from the school about this?"

"I have no *fucking* idea, but I'll be down at the school Monday morning to find out."

Jane sighed deeply as she kept her hand over her mouth. "Oh God, Matt, Rich and Scarlett. I can't imagine how they feel."

"No, neither can I. I feel terrible."

"I'm going to call her."

I looked at the clock and was surprised to see that it was only nine. Winter nights seemingly never end. "Put it on speaker. I want to make sure they know we're both with them."

The phone rang multiple times before Scarlett picked up. Her voice juxtaposed what I expected. "Hey lady, getting kind of late. Aren't you usually in bed by now?"

The tone of her voice threw us both for a loop, but we grounded ourselves and pushed forward, thinking she must be putting on a strong face for our sake. "Scar, we're so sorry. Is there anything you need?"

Scarlett gave an unsure, quick laugh. "What do you mean? Sarah said the party was great. Sorry we couldn't stay. We had so much running around to do."

We both looked at each other as a sudden, horrific realization crept over us. Sarah hadn't told them. Our voices collectively stumbled over themselves. We could actually hear Scarlett sit up further and lean into the phone.

"Jane, what are you talking about? You're scaring me."

Jane's mouth refused to work, but I knew that sitting in silence on the phone would only add to Scarlett's stress. "Scar, it's Matt. Um, listen, Laura told us something tonight. Something about Sarah that I'm afraid you might not know. Something that you need to know. Is Rich there?"

A gruff voice spoke from somewhere a bit far away from the phone's speaker. "Yeah, Matt. I'm here. What's going on?"

I sighed and ran my fingers through my hair. Jane looked at me with eyes that became wetter by the moment. "Listen, um, Laura told us about something that happened at school. Something that involved one of the faculty members. Have you guys heard this yet?"

I could see the scene in their home as though I was there. Scarlett looking at Rich, shaking her head, and Rich making his way over to the couch to sit next to her. His voice was a lot closer when he spoke next.

"We haven't heard from the school, no. What did Laura say?"

"I don't know how to say this, guys, so I'm just going to come out with it." I paused only for a moment to calm the wavering of my voice. "Laura said that one of the janitors at the school…well, he was fired the other day because, as she put it, he was watching Sarah while she…when she was in the bathroom."

Scarlett immediately began sobbing, which caused Jane, who had been fighting tears off with all her willpower, to break down as well. No one spoke on their side of the phone for a solid minute.

When Rich spoke, it was evident that he was fighting a lump in his own throat. "How's that, Matt? I mean, how did Laura know this? We haven't heard anything about it."

"Well, to be honest, we only just found out ourselves. When I was putting Laura down, she seemed out of sorts. I asked her what was wrong, and she was really evasive. But she finally told me.

"There was some guy that had walked by the house when the kids were all playing in the living room. The wind was howling and blowing snow against the window, so they had all run over to look. God, Rich, now that I think of it, Sarah had turned away and went back to playing almost immediately while the other kids looked."

Scarlett spoke in a broken voice. "A guy, Matt. You said there was a guy?"

"Yeah, I didn't see anyone at first, just the kids gathered around. But when they all went back to playing, Laura stayed, looking outside. When she started waving, a cautious wave, mind you, not a wave you'd expect a kid to give to a friend, I got up. By the time I was at the window, his back was turned, and he was making his way down the road. I never got a good look." I paused, letting this information sink in before continuing.

"Laura said that man used to work at the school. She said that Sarah had told her a secret that she didn't want to tell. I convinced her that if Sarah was in trouble, she really needed to tell someone."

"Oh, God," Scarlett said through choked sobs.

Rich's response was one of anger more than sadness. "That fucking school. How could this happen? How could no one have contacted us? How the fuck—"

"Rich," Scarlett snapped, "getting this angry isn't helping right now. We need to make sure Sarah is okay." Her attention turned back to the phone. "Jane, Matt, thank you for calling. Sarah only just went to bed. I think we're going to go in and talk to her. If there is anything else you find out…" She began crying again, a light, pained sound that she was clearly trying to keep under control.

"Of course, Scar. We'll keep you in the loop. I'm so sorry for all this."

Scarlett had already made her way down the hall. Jane got up and made her way to Laura's room, clearly needing to just sit in her presence for a bit. Whether Laura was still awake or not, I didn't know.

"Matt, you still there?" I took the phone off speaker and held it to my ear.

"Yeah, still here, Rich. Jeez, we really are sorry about this. If there is anything—"

Rich cut me off, "Yes, thanks, Matt. Really. I'm just so mad I could…I could. *Fuck.*" He breathed angrily through his teeth.

"I know, Rich. I can only imagine."

"You said you couldn't get a good look at him? You saw nothing?"

"Nothing that is going to help identify him, Rich. No. Jeans and a hoodie. That's all."

Rich sighed deeply, and I heard ice cubes clinking in a glass of what I assumed was some top-shelf whiskey, a favorite of myself and Rich. "Alright, I need to go sit with my little girl. We'll chat tomorrow, yes?"

"Absolutely, my friend. Head high tonight. Hold each other a little closer."

"We'll do that. Goodnight, Matt."

"Goodnight, Rich."

I ended the call and looked down the hall. Laura's light was on, clearly awake and talking to Jane. I imagined the fear Sarah must have felt. The anxiety Laura must have felt keeping Sarah's secret.

She did the right thing by telling me. We did the right thing by telling Rich and Scar, I thought.

"Dad," Laura called from her room.

"I'm coming, baby."

Chapter 15

I tossed and turned the remainder of the night but I did eventually fall asleep to the white noise of the wind as the storm traveled far to our east. As I slowly woke, I became aware of the smell of grass drying in the rising sun. Birds chirped in the distance as I opened my eyes to the blinding white light that filled the tent.

I sat up and noticed the tent flap open, the girl already in the field snacking on a granola bar that she must have gotten from the bottom of my pack. She was dressed in her same clothes and I thought, as she sat in the middle of the field, taking in the sun as it rose higher in the morning sky, that she must be still drying them out.

I saw my pants and shirt in the corner of the tent and was shocked to feel that, though they were in a ball the remainder of the night, they were surprisingly dry already. Perhaps it was later than I thought, and the sun had dried them throughout the morning, though I didn't think so. I stood, hunched over in the tent, and put my pants on, choosing instead to step outside of the tent to deal with the shirt. The grass was a pillow under my aching feet. We had already done a lot of walking, and we had even further to go today. Food was dwindling, and we were going to start losing energy if we didn't find our way out of the woods soon.

The girl saw me exit the tent and smiled a huge toothy grin, waving me over. I looked down at my boots but couldn't resist the feeling of the grass between my toes. The soft tickle of the blades between my toes rejuvenated me, getting me ready for the long day ahead. When I got to her and sat down, she handed me the rest of the granola bar and laid back, face to the sky.

"Today is going to be a good day," she said.

I smiled, hoping what she said was true. "Oh, yeah? Why do you think that?"

She tilted her head toward me as I bit into the bar. "I just know. We're close to one of my favorite places. We'll stop there when we get there."

My eagerness to get out of the forest was immense, but I felt as though I couldn't deny her this. She needed to remain calm, and if stopping somewhere for a little while would give her a morale boost, I saw no reason why a short stop couldn't happen.

The granola bar tasted delicious but tore lightly at my throat as it went down without a chaser. "We need to find some water."

"Oh, that's easy," she said. "Right over that way is a stream we can use."

The thought of a cool drink enthused me, but the fear of catching giardia or some other waterborne illness made me hesitate. *Maybe if the water was moving fast enough.* The girl sat up as though reading my thoughts clearly.

"You do have that straw in your pack, remember?"

She was right. She must have seen my life straw when she was getting the granola bar. The life straw that I always carried with me. How stupid was I to forget? The straw allowed you to drink from even the dirtiest of water sources and be relatively confident that you would not find yourself hunched over a fallen tree in the woods, with diarrhea from one end and vomit from the other. It didn't do much for the taste, though.

I smiled. "Care to show me to the stream?"

She jumped right up and held her hand out to me as though she'd be able to lift me with no effort. "Right this way."

I walked over to my pack, grabbed the straw and water bottle, and followed her, hand in hand, into the woods.

She was right. Only a few yards into the tree line, behind where we had set our tent up, lay a stream that was moving at a faster pace than I would have imagined for a body of water so small.

Remember the storm last night? Of course, it must be the deluge from last night that caused the strange pace of this would-be river.

The girl went downstream, where the flow slowed a bit from the rocks that rose above the water. She dipped her still bare feet in and laughed at the sensation of the water trying to push her from them. She kicked and almost slipped, my heart jumping as I took an immediate step in her direction before she steadied herself and came back to the shore.

She sat on a patch of grass that appeared, somehow, to have remained fairly dry, though the waves the rocks created as the water cascaded over them did their best to saturate as far onto the land as they could. I stepped out into the river and dipped my bottle into the cold water. Cold was a bit of an understatement. It was almost frigid. A reminder that, even though the sun was warm on our faces, the mountains were still preparing for winter. I stuck the straw in the bottle and sucked down a long swallow, the chill coating my throat and rinsing away any granola that held on against the free fall into my gut. I dipped the bottle back in once more, filling it to the brim, before walking over to the girl who was throwing pebbles in and laughing at the *blub* sound as they sunk beneath the surface.

I held out the bottle, and she smiled, grabbing it and taking a long drink from the straw, as well. She handed me back the bottle and looked at me, a question clearly just behind her lips.

"Matt," she hesitated, "do you have a family?"

When I looked at her, I saw the loneliness that was hidden just beyond her childlike stare, and my mind wondered once more how it was possible for someone so young to be lost for so long and yet still survive.

And then I remembered the being that I had seen the previous night. The being that had so frightened me and yet had regarded the girl with such gentleness and caring. I didn't know how such a thing might have existed, but I knew what I had seen, and I knew what the girl had told me. She said there were others, and I thought about all the unexplored parts of the world, seemingly smaller each day but yet still existing. People report every year that they see Bigfoot, and I had no trouble believing most of their stories. Why was I having trouble believing what my eyes had shown me? If I believe a family of Bigfoot can live undetected in nature, why not a family of these beings?

If that being had frightened me, the being that had apparently befriended and cared for this child while she survived in the wild, the beast that I saw as I zipped up the tent chilled me to the bone. I had only seen it—or thought I saw it—for a moment, but that was long enough to send my stomach rolling inside with even the slightest recollection of it in my mind. I wondered if that was the thing that I saw stalking me on the trail when the girl had disappeared. If so, I worried even more. This thing was here, and it wasn't leaving. She knew it, and now I did as well.

I smiled quickly, pushing my fears aside and answering her. "I do. I have a wife and a daughter. I'd say my daughter is a little younger than you."

She smiled, and I thought she might have been swallowing a wave of emotion. After a moment, she cleared her throat. "Can you tell me about her? Your daughter, I mean."

Thinking about Laura pulled at my heart but brought me joy as well. "Well, Laura just turned seven. She's got brown hair that she likes to wear in a ponytail and freckles that like to show themselves during the warm weather. She's short for her age; people sometimes think she's only about five, but she's smart and does better than almost all the kids in her class.

"She's very into dolls. Stuffed, plastic, fabric, it doesn't matter. There are dolls everywhere. They all have names, and they all have their own personalities. I'm telling you, her imagination is amazing. I tell my wife all the time, Jane, she's going to be a writer someday. The stories she creates when she's playing…" I paused, my mind drifting to a place far from here. A place where Jane, Laura, and I were all curled up on the couch by the fire, eating popcorn and watching a movie. A place that feels lost. "I hope you get to meet her someday when we get out of here."

The girl smiled weakly and pulled her knees to her chest. "She sounds very nice. I would like to meet her someday."

"Well, then it's settled. When we get out of here, I will make sure your parents have my number, and we will get you two together as soon as possible."

The girl laid back on the pillowy grass, her knotted hair flattening underneath the weight of her head. There was a soft breaking of branches from across the stream, and for a moment, I feared the evil thing that lurked in the shadows would be staring at us, preparing to attack, but instead, a doe stood several yards away. Her tan fur shone in the sunlight that was able to penetrate the canopy of trees above. Her tongue licked the air. Her nose sensed our presence even before her eyes did. She froze instinctually, assessing us and how much of a threat we imposed.

"Tell me about your wife, Jane, right?" the girl said softly, now sitting up and watching the deer with curiosity and wonder.

"Jane, well, what do you want to know?"

She thought briefly. "How did you meet?"

I chuckled as I remembered how my heart had skipped when she walked into my classroom. "She was a teacher at the school I work at."

"Was?" the girl asked.

"Mm-hm. She quit when we decided to have children. I told her she didn't have to, but…well, we lost the first pregnancy. So, when she got pregnant a second time, Jane wanted to be sure she was always right there. Didn't want to be burdened with everything that teachers have to do."

She nodded again, listening, but somewhere far away as well. "What is she like?"

I thought back to her gentle kisses, the way her perfume hung in the room after she left, and the way her body curved into mine when we lay snuggling in bed. I ached to hold her again. She must be worried to death about me at this point. She would surely have reported me missing, but it wouldn't do much good. I was carried, who knows how far down river, and walked equally that distance in the other direction in an attempt to get myself out. No, the Rangers would likely never find me. The girl and I were on our own, and it was up to us to find our way to safety.

"She's, well, she's kind. One second of hearing her voice would convince you of that. It's soft…pure. I can listen to her talk after a long day and feel myself relaxing. I think it's the voice that a mother naturally gets when she spends most of her day talking to a cooing baby."

The doe determined that we were no threat and made her way past several downed trees in the direction of a patch of grass that she'd use as breakfast. Her ears flicked away several flies as she made sure to still be aware of our presence.

"She's beautiful."

"The deer or your wife?" the girl asked with a smirk on her face.

I looked at her and smiled genuinely. "Both, I suppose. Hey, we should probably get going. We have a long walk ahead of us."

"Just a few more minutes. I just want to know a little more about her. Is that okay?"

I hesitated, knowing we had a lot of miles to go to be anywhere near where the girl had pointed the previous day, but in the end, I relented. "Of course."

She turned her whole body to face me, and I did the same.

"She loves music," I said. "She is always singing and dancing around the house. If Laura is around, she'll join in. It seems as though there is always some song playing throughout the house, not that I mind. But sometimes, I do enjoy a bit of quiet. That's why I come out to the woods." I looked around. "Maybe I have to reassess that when I get home."

"No, don't do that. You love it out here. This is just a setback. You'll see, when we get out of here, the woods will call you back. They offer you clarity. Life just gets messy sometimes."

Once again, I was struck by the girl's profound reasoning. *How did she become so insightful so young?*

"Maybe you're right. Oh, one other thing about Jane. She can't read to herself. She always has to speak the words out loud, even if it's just a dull whisper. I asked her once why she did that, and she told me it was because she was never able to concentrate on books when she was younger. Her house was always so loud. So she would say the words out loud and be better able to concentrate. I guess it makes sense if you think about it."

"It does," she said as she stood up. "She sounds like my mom."

"Your mom?" I was thrilled that the girl was finally willing to open up to me a bit.

"Yeah, I listened to so many stories when she thought I wasn't paying attention because she did the same thing. My favorite was when she talked really quietly. It could put me to sleep if I let it."

I rose and dusted the seat of my pants off. "It sounds like your mom is going to have a new friend when we get out of here, too."

"I hope so," she said as she walked back in the direction of our camp.

Chapter 16

Hours sluggishly passed as we marched our way north, then west, then north again. The sun, low in the east when we began our day's walk, now sat in the western sky. Our steps had become monotonous hours ago, and our conversation had waned. Only the occasional drink of water brought any break-up to the day's long march.

The day had started off warm by the stream. The air light and easy to breathe. By midday, the sun's constant assault had become tiring, but it was nothing compared to the humidity that seemed to spring up out of nowhere. What I wouldn't have given to have a cold breeze come upon us, like jumping into a pool on a hot summer day—refreshing.

My pack weighed on me as heavy as ever. I actually seriously considered dumping most of it but thought better of it. First, I couldn't bring myself to litter in the forest. "Leave No Trace." Secondly, I knew that as soon as I left something, we would need it. I simply couldn't risk it. I would bear the weight, and we would get out of here.

To the girl's credit, she seemed unphased by the temperature change. True that she wasn't moving quite as fast as the day before, and her hair was matted to her head with sweat, but she spent no time complaining and walked confidently in the direction of our escape.

As I offered her the last sip from the bottle, I heard the distinct sound of water cascading over a drop of some height. I had never been much of a religious man, but at that moment, I was convinced that something out there must have been looking out for us. That is until I saw what stood between us and our respite.

The girl led the way off the trail and through a wide copse, the cascading water sounding closer with each step. My legs ached, and my feet throbbed, but I pushed myself on, imagining the cold water massaging the pain away. I could literally feel my body cooling off with no more than the thought of submerging myself in the water's depths.

A river appeared next to us, different than the one I had fallen in I assumed, given how far away we were from my accident, its water moving with a ferocity I had not expected. Our path was taking us downhill gradually, but we found ourselves staring over a forty-foot cliff of sheer granite. My heart sank.

"Damn, I was really hoping to get in that water," I said miserably.

"That's where we're going. Down there," the girl said as she scanned the cliff's edge. "Remember, I told you that I had somewhere I wanted to show you."

I looked at her, confused. "You want us to get down there? How do you propose we do that?"

She sat down, her legs dangling off the edge. "We climb down."

I let out a frantic laugh. I couldn't help myself. Fear of the situation and the complete insanity of her plan was just too much. "Come on," I said as I began walking back up the hill, still snickering. "We need to get back on the trail. The sun is already starting to fade."

"Matt," she said with no hint of sarcasm. "This is the way."

My frustration was mounting. The heat and humidity had worn me down all day. I had no patience for this insanity. "Kid, there is no way to get down that. It's too high to jump and too sheer to climb. We'll fall. We'll die."

"No, we won't. I've climbed this a lot of times. Come here and look, it's not that scary. There are places to put your feet. Places to hold onto."

Beside myself, I walked as close to the edge as I dared before getting on my knees and crawling the rest of the way. There were indeed small outcroppings that scattered the otherwise sheer wall, but they were hardly big enough for her feet, let alone my own. I pushed myself away from the edge and begged her to come away from it as well, shaking my head.

Through the fog of fear, my mind drifted back to that day, all those years ago, standing at the bottom of the ladders on Mount Morgan. Looking up, about the same height as lay before us now—only now I was at the top; I thought there was no way I could do it. The ladders were scary but doable. Swinging my legs over the drop and holding on to the ladder on the far side of it seemed impossible. Yet, I did it. Maybe I could do this, too?

The fear started to release its tight grip on me. Somewhere in the back of my mind, I heard my father telling me that it's not impossible; it can be done. The girl sat looking at me, my eyes still a bit wild, and seemed to contemplate what to say. She had claimed to have climbed this before, and if she could, I surely could. Right?

I edged my way slowly to the precipice, this time on my butt rather than my belly. The girl watched me, unsure what to expect from me as I contemplated my next move. I steeled myself enough to let my legs dangle next to hers, though I leaned back against my outstretched arms, balancing myself away from the drop. She smiled and put her hand lightly on my back.

"See, it's not so bad."

"You've done this before?" I confirmed before making my final determination.

"Mm-hmm. And when we're at the bottom, we'll be able to get in that water and cool off. "You'll be out of here tomorrow."

"I'll be out of here tomorrow? You will be, too, you know?"

The girl just nodded her head and breathed a low sigh. "Come on, let's get down there."

The revelation that we were almost out was all I needed to get moving. I clenched my teeth and turned on all fours, my back now to the drop. "I'll go first. You come once I'm far enough down for you to start."

My foot reached for some hold but found nothing but open air. My entire body tensed as I imagined myself falling like I did before. Only this time, I wouldn't be falling into a river. My body would be shattered among the rocks that lay below. A fleeting thought of not dying on impact crossed my mind. My body crumbled in a heap, unable to move, blood pooling around my head.

Then, my foot found purchase. I dared to let myself lean further onto it, suddenly feeling more confident in the climb down. I was shocked to find that almost my entire boot was able to fit on this ledge. I looked at the girl who just gave me a confident smile, urging me forward. Slowly, carefully, I brought my other leg over the edge and almost immediately found a hold for myself again. With both my feet standing on footholds that seemed safe, my confidence rose once more. I thought that I must not have been close enough to the edge to see these for the width that they were when I had crawled over so tentatively.

I made my way further down, my head now below where the girl sat. She looked down at me and turned around, preparing to make her descent. The climb turned out to be extremely smooth, and when I allowed myself to drop the final five feet or so to the rocky ground, I let out a holler of excitement. I knew I was running on pure adrenaline, but I felt alive.

I stepped back so that the girl could drop down in front of me. Like a gymnast, she dismounted the rock wall and spun toward me, her hand thrust out for a high five. I obliged before she ran down the hill toward the crystal blue pool of water below.

We had dipped our toes in the water earlier that day, but that was nothing compared to the sensation of walking into the cold pool that formed beneath the waterfall. I had stripped down to my boxer shorts and cautiously made my way into the water, deciding another night of soaked clothes was not for me. The girl laughed on the bank as my knees went under, freezing me in place as my arms instinctually crossed over my chest.

The waterfall stood to my right, white water cascading over the ledge and crashing among the rocks at the bottom. The sound was thunderous. It had been so quiet most of the day as we death marched through the woods that the sound of the water (and the cold water itself) threatened a headache that I could not much afford. My feet had gone numb when I heard the girl behind me.

"Hey, Matt."

I turned and saw that she was standing directly behind me, her shorts partially submerged already, the dirt turning the water a cloudy brown. She smiled wryly at me…and pushed me.

I gasped and tried desperately to find footing beneath the water but my foot only found a slick rock that was resting diagonally; no help at all. My toes grabbed at nothing, and I fell backward, finding myself completely underwater.

I panicked.

The feeling of being under, the cold emptiness wrapping itself around me, the sound of the waterfall, then and now, stunned me. I reached out my leg, sure that I would find the bottom just below me. I felt nothing. The river bottom dropped off quickly and though I knew how to swim well, my limbs seemed to not want to cooperate. I felt like I was sinking. A rock thrown from the shore.

It's funny how time plays tricks when you are scared. If you asked me then, I would have said I was drowning for minutes. Looking back on it, I was likely only under for seconds.

Finally, my brain sent the right signals to my limbs, and I waved my arms frantically. My legs followed suit, and I made my way to the bank, furious. Fear takes on different forms depending on the circumstance.

I wiped the water from my eyes, rubbing my palms against them to clear my vision, red-faced from the cold and anger. I heard her before I saw her.

She was laughing. A laughter of pure childlike innocence. When I opened my eyes, she was half-sitting-half-lying in the water, head tilted back to the sky, laughing so hard that, at times, no sound came out at all. She kicked her feet up and down, splashing the water onto the embankment.

"That…was…so…funny," she wheezed out between breaths.

My anger quickly subsided when I saw the unabashed delight lighting up her face. The water dripped from my hair and onto my back and chest, keeping the goosebumps like hills rising off the plains.

When she finally got herself under control, she stood knee-deep in the water and turned to me. Her face sank when she saw the scowl that I had kept on my own, though my heart had softened, realizing her playful gesture. I walked slowly toward her like a predator stalking prey. She lowered her head and, thinking I was mad at her, tried to stammer out an apology.

I held up my hand. "Hey…guess what?"

She raised her eyes once more, a questioning look crossing her sweet face.

I closed the last few feet quickly and scooped her up in my arms, a squeal of joy that could have started as fear escaping her. I carried her a few feet further into the water and looked at her in my arms as she realized what I was about to do.

"Can you swim?"

Her smile blocked out the sun. "Like a fish."

Like salmon swimming upstream, I launched her through the air. She reached up and plugged her nose a fraction of a second before she disappeared beneath the water. Now I was laughing, a full-bellied laugh that only one without a care in the world can muster.

And at that moment, standing there under the warm sun in the cold water, I had not a single care in the world.

We played for what felt like hours in that pool. We even swam over to the waterfall and let it rain down upon our heads, the pressure almost too much to handle. Tiny fish swam below us, and butterflies flapped their wings above. The time we spent at that pool was serenity and when I look back at it, I realize I had grown to love that little girl.

How was it possible to feel so strongly for this child that I had just met? Perhaps it was simply an emotional response that sprung from the depths of my being due to the longing for Laura. Perhaps it was more? Either way, I longed for her safety and mine as well. I longed to hear her laugh the way she did in the water. I vowed at that moment, splashing under the waterfall, that I would protect her even at the cost of my own life. I had no will to die. No. In fact, my desire to get home to my family rested squarely in the center of my mind at all times. But, this child would be safe with me. She would know no fear with me by her side.

As she sat on the banks of the river, I set up the tent far enough back to not be assaulted by the mist from the waterfall all night. She tossed stones into the water and tried once or twice to skip them over the surface. I smiled, remembering when I taught Laura to do the same.

By the time the tent was up (it always took me longer than I expected to get the tent situated) and I had gotten a fire roaring, the sun had dipped behind the horizon. The girl sat close to the fire, drying her clothes and her skin while I walked over to my pack, desperately hoping there was still something at the bottom for us to eat, though knowing in my heart there was nothing more than a few peanut butter crackers.

When I got within a few feet of where I had laid the pack before jumping in the water, I noticed that it was gone once more. I found it several yards away, sitting upright against a tall oak tree whose width almost hid the bag entirely. I scanned the area, suddenly very aware of the nightfall rapidly approaching and remembering the being I had seen the previous night.

The woods blackened not far from where I stood, but there was no sign of anyone or anything watching us. I grabbed the pack by one of its deep red straps and moved away from the darkening area as quickly as I could, back toward the fire.

I noticed the pack felt a bit heavier than it had earlier in the day, unusual considering how tired I had been from our hike and the sun beating down upon us. The girl sat with her legs stretched out in front of her, toes toward the fire, looking at me expectantly. Knowingly. I sat the bag down between us and groaned as I lowered myself.

"So," she asked, "what's for dinner?"

I sighed, knowing that we'd be going mostly hungry tonight. I considered diving back into the water and attempting to catch one of the little fish we had seen earlier but dismissed the idea quickly. Who did I think I was? Plus, with the setting sun, it had become a lot cooler, and the water was already cold enough.

"I hate to break it to you, kid. But I think we're only snacking on a few crackers tonight."

"You sure?" she said coyly. "I really think we had more than that in there." She pushed the bag toward me. "Check it out."

I sighed and put the bag in my lap, slowly unzipping it. My eyes widened when I saw two fresh hunks of meat lying right on top. It looked like deer meat, but I supposed it could be a moose or even a bear. I didn't really care; it was meat, and it appeared fresh.

"Wait…"

The girl just looked at me. "I told you, he's good. He takes care of me."

I remembered her story. She told me that this being had protected her, kept her safe, since she had been in this place. It must have come while we were distracted in the water. It gave me chills imagining it watching us from the tree line. Seeing our playful behavior all while, what? Killing a being and stuffing chunks of its flesh into my pack. I shook my head and realized that however strange it felt to me, this girl knew her *friend* far better than I did. It was best for me to just accept this gift and rest with a full belly.

I reached my arm out to the girl with my empty water bottle. "Go fill us up, please."

We lay under the night sky, gazing at the sparkles high above. The two of us lay side-by-side, our stomachs full and our hearts happy. It had been a good day, a long day (my feet were still throbbing slightly), but it had ended as well as one could imagine out here. We spoke no words, just stared at the stars shimmering high above us.

I turned my head to the right, high above the waterfall, which had slowed a bit in the time we had spent there, and pointed to the sky. "Oh, wow, look at that."

The girl turned her head and, for the first time since we finished eating, sat up, her eyes wide with fascination. "What is that?"

"It's a comet, I think. It's strange, though; it's moving, but it's far too slow to be a shooting star."

She looked at me, confused. "A shooting star?"

I smiled. "Yes. A shooting star is a piece of a meteor…a rock in outer space. When it comes close to Earth, it starts to burn up in the atmosphere. Shooting stars happen all the time, but they are so quick, only a second or two at most, that most people don't even see them." I looked back up to the large red object moving slowly above us. "Whatever that is is far too slow to be that."

The girl hadn't taken her eyes off the object since I noticed it. "Do you think there are other people that live up there?"

I thought about it for a moment. Up until a few days ago, I would have thought it unlikely. But now, having seen what I'd seen in these woods, I wondered. "I'm not sure. I mean, it's an awfully big place up there. Maybe. Maybe there is."

The girl nodded. "I think there is."

"Oh yeah? What makes you so sure?"

"Well, there are things here that we don't even understand." She took her eyes away from the red object and looked at me. "Even you. You saw my friend and can't understand what he is."

I chuckled. "Well, that is for sure."

"See, and we live here." She looked back up to the sky. "There are so many stars. So many chances for…for people. Don't you think?"

I let my eyes wander back up and thought about what she was saying. Once again, I found myself awestruck by the girl. "I think you might be right."

"Oh, I know I am." She smiled her playful smile at me. "I bet that big red thing is some people traveling right now."

I couldn't help but laugh at her. I couldn't tell if she was being serious or having some fun. "Well, if it is, I bet they are wondering what kind of a trash pit they are flying by now."

"Oh, come on," she spoke with a tone of seriousness. "It's not all that bad."

I lowered my eyes. "You haven't seen enough of the world yet. Stay young, if not in body, in your heart."

She stood up and stretched, and a yawn passed from her to me. "I'm never going to grow up, don't worry."

The naivety of a child.

"How about we climb into the tent and get some shut-eye?"

"Sure, I'm just going to go pee. I'll be back."

I rose from my comfy spot on the grass and brushed myself off before making my way over to the tent, black and ominous looking just outside the reach of the flames of the fire. As I lay down, I could hear the girl whispering a short distance off. I had suspected she was going to do more than use the bathroom. The zipper of the tent was still open, so I stuck my head out quietly.

"I know…" she whispered, though I could not see her or the being she was talking to. "I'll tell him more. I'm remembering now."

I decided to give her the privacy she deserved and laid back down. My eyes were heavy, and by the time the girl had crawled in next to me, I was only semi-awake.

"Are you still up?" she asked in a quiet voice.

I grumbled but rolled to my side to face her, my eyes were slits that didn't want to fully open.

"I was hoping we could talk a bit more."

"Do you think we could talk a bit more in the morning? I'm really tired."

Even though my eyes had closed once more, I could hear the disappointment in her voice.

"Sure, in the morning. Goodnight, Matt."

"Goodnight."

"Riley."

My eyes opened slowly, her back turned to me.

"Riley?" I asked.

"That's my name, Matt. Riley. I'm sorry I didn't tell you sooner."

"You're remembering things," I said as happily as I could muster.

"Mm-hmm," she mumbled, "and soon, you will too."

I lay next to her for quite a while, contemplating what she thought I needed to remember. I didn't understand the things I had seen in my short time with her, but I knew exactly what I needed to do—get out and get back to Jane and Laura. I smiled as I remembered the little girl, Riley, telling me that we would be out of the woods tomorrow. Our time together was almost over.

Her sudden snores coerced my eyes to close once more, and as the fire faded away outside, the red comet and the white moon fought for supremacy over the night sky.

Chapter 17

Laura's official birthday came in like a whisper. Jane had woken up early to make Laura's favorite breakfast—homemade French toast, bacon, and some sausage patties—but when Laura came out of her room and sat at the table, her eyes remained low, and her usually exuberant demeanor was muted against the sunny morning.

When I finally made my way down to the kitchen, after jumping in the shower and throwing on my Patriots jersey, I found my wife sitting next to her, a hand on her back, and leaned in close, talking quietly. I knew why Laura was so down this year. I knew it was because of what her best friend had gone through. With her telling me last night, all those fears were real again, the feelings needing to be addressed.

I also knew not to interrupt the quiet conversations between mother and daughter, and so I silently made my way to the coffee pot and then to the living room couch, where I turned on *Sportscenter* and hoped to get some information to sure up my fantasy football lineup, knowing I would likely not be able to watch too much that day.

Several minutes later, Jane plopped down next to me, a deep sigh escaping her. I immediately tensed, afraid of what she might tell me. I looked over my shoulder and back to the empty kitchen.

"Where's Laura?"

"She went back to her room to lie down. She's really worried about going back to school tomorrow."

I dipped my head. "I can imagine."

"What are we going to do, Matt? She's scared to death. She told me that she thought that man had been watching her, too. Not in the bathroom, but in the halls. She's seen him at recess staring at her, too."

My blood ran cold. I found myself clenching my fists as she talked, furious at the ineptitude of the school for not doing something sooner—feeling the ineptitude in myself for not being able to protect her.

"We're going to go down to the school tomorrow morning and have a real serious conversation with the principal. That's a start, at least."

"I was thinking we should invite Rich and Scar out to dinner tonight. Obviously, Sarah, too. I think it'll do the girls some good to have some alone time, and the adults can all talk about the game plan for Monday morning."

I nodded. "Yeah, that's a good plan. Let's do it. You want to give them a call?"

"Yeah, I'll call. While I'm doing that, why don't you go say happy birthday to your daughter."

"Shit, I saw you two talking, and I didn't want to interrupt. I'm an idiot."

"You're not an idiot," she said as she pulled out her phone. "You're just a father with a lot on his mind right now."

I gave her a kiss on the cheek. "Thanks, babe." I got up and made my way down the hall.

The more I thought about it, the angrier I got. We lived in a quiet, rural community. In the type of neighborhood where the kids are always outside and Saturday mornings are spent mowing your lawn and hedging the bushes, maybe pulling weeds from your walkway or garden. Kids weren't supposed to be afraid there; they were meant to thrive here, to live their best lives.

I had not been a fan of the way the education system was progressing in this country for a long time. Standards-based grading, no deadlines for work, papers being handed in whenever the student decided to do them, but all that was outside of this. Beyond the boundaries of whether or not a child subjectively passed a subject or not. This was neglect. This was reckless at best. How could they let someone like this into the school? What was the vetting process for getting staff hired? These were questions that I needed answers to and I'm sure only the tip of the iceberg for Rich and Scar.

I knocked on Laura's closed door. "Can I come in?"

A quiet *sure* came from within. I pushed the door open slowly and saw my daughter lying in her bed with one of her dolls in the crook of her arm, just staring at the ceiling. Her eyes were still wet, and though she tried to hide her tears, the streaks stood out on her cheeks.

I am a firm believer that there is nothing worse in this world than seeing your child in emotional pain. Trying to stop your kids from getting physically hurt is typically an exercise in futility. Bumps, bruises, scratches, hell, even a broken bone now and then can be accepted and dealt with. But the emotional pain of one so young is simply heart-wrenching.

I walked over to her bed and sat on the end, unsure of what to say to make her feel better. "So, are you excited for *Yummy Burger* tonight?"

She shrugged, indifferent to the idea of her favorite place to go eat. "I guess."

"Oh, you'll love it. You always do," I said with a feigned sense of happiness, a somewhat poor effort to make her smile. "Besides, Mom's calling Sarah's parents right now. Sarah is probably coming, too. Just you two tonight."

She looked down at me sitting on the end of her bed, the movement of her head jarring loose a single tear. "But, Dad, Sarah is going to be mad at me. I told her secret. I don't want her to come."

"Aw, Laura, Sarah is not going to be mad at you. You are protecting her. She's going to know that. She would have done the same thing for you. Would you be mad at her if she told her parents a secret in order to make sure you were safe?"

She thought about this momentarily and then shook her head and turned onto her side. I moved closer to her and placed my hand in the center of her back.

"Hey, we can't have you so upset on your big day. Is there anything I can do to make you feel better?"

She was quiet for a long time before answering. "No. Not right now. I just want to be alone in here for a little bit."

My heart broke a little more, but I wanted to respect her feelings. I stood up and leaned over to kiss the top of her head. "I love you, Laura. Happy birthday." I made my way over to her door, and as I was closing it, she spoke.

"I love you too, Dad."

When the door latched behind me, I made my way into the bathroom and stared at myself in the mirror, fighting away my own tears that threatened to rain down.

An hour later Jane came out of Laura's room, the two dressed in warm sweaters and jeans, a slight smile across our daughter's face. Jane always seemed to know what to do; I often felt at a loss, always wanting to do the right thing but fumbling around to find the words.

"And where are you two heading looking so pretty?"

"Well, Laura and I decided to go have a girls' day. We're going to go get our hair and nails done," she walked closer and kissed me, whispering in my ear, "and do our best to forget about this whole ugly situation for a few hours."

"I think that's great, honey. You two will have a great day. You sure you don't want me to come."

"We're sure, Dad. This is a girls-only day."

I smiled, shocked to see the transformation that occurred while Jane was behind closed doors. I marveled at how she did it. "Okay, ladies. But don't fill up on lunch. Remember, *Yummy Burger* tonight."

"We promise. Rich, Scar, and Sarah will meet us there at around six. We'll be home well before that."

The girls put on their coats, gloves, and boots and opened the front door, letting the frigid January air blow tiny flakes of snow into the living room. I shivered in my Tom Brady jersey and thought that I was glad I'd be staying in the warmth of the house today. We exchanged kisses and hugs, and the girls left. I watched them both as they got into the car and drove down the road. A warmth that wasn't entirely from the heaters overcame me. I went to the kitchen, grabbed a soda and a bag of chips, sat down, and watched the pre-game playoff show as they showed the Patriots warming up on the field.

I was riding high when the girls walked back in the door an hour before we had to leave. The Patriots had dominated the game from start to finish, and now the hated Cowboys were getting shellacked by the San Francisco 49ers. It was turning out to be quite a good day.

Laura came rushing into the house, threw her boots to the side, and ran over to me, jumping onto the couch.

"Dad, look at my nails! What do you think?"

They were a beautiful shade of green and had little dots of color on each—what looked to be Christmas lights; the season might have passed, but it was still Laura's favorite.

"They are beautiful. And look at your hair. They really did a great job."

"She's been so excited to come show you," Jane said from the still-opened doorway.

"Everything really does look great, Laura. You are beautiful." I let my eyes drift to the window and saw that pink clouds hung in the sky as the sun was setting rapidly on the horizon. I walked over to greet Jane as Laura ran down the hall toward the bathroom. "Mmm, you look great, too," I said quietly as I kissed her neck.

Jane leaned into me but had her hands against my chest, not letting me get as close as I wanted to. She had a new scent on her, one I didn't recognize but was enthralled with.

"What are you wearing?"

"Just something new I thought I'd try. We found it at one of the stores downtown." Her words showed no distress, but her eyes held something behind them.

"What's wrong?"

"Nothing. Just something that happened while we were out. It's not a big deal."

"Jane, what happened? Laura seems fine. Better than fine, actually."

"No, no. It's not Laura. Just some creep had to make some shitty comment."

"What do you mean?" I asked, caution growing within me.

Jane had taken her outerwear off and was walking toward the couch. She sighed deeply and spoke. "We had just gotten out of the salon, and Laura was a few feet ahead of me. She was heading toward the toy store when some guy walked by me and said…" She paused and rolled her head back against the pillow on the couch.

"What?" My blood pressure was rising again.

"He said something along the lines of how good I looked. Something about the hair between my legs being trimmed as nicely as the hair on my head."

I heard the bathroom door open down the hall and it took every ounce of willpower to not rise off the couch and hurl obscenities to the sky. Why did some men think it was okay to speak to women like this? What was the point?

I knew the point. The point was that these men got off on the power. They got off on making women feel self-conscious. They thought that it made them more, that it made them bigger. It was disgusting. The world had always been a dangerous place for women, but it seemed to be getting worse by the day. Rapes, assault, kidnapping. Every day, the news showed some new story about a woman being murdered by her jealous boyfriend, a stalker, or some young girl being trafficked for the profit of some filth who thought it was his right to take her body. As a father, as a husband, it was terrifying to not be around, protecting them at all times. Lord knows I am no fighter, but oftentimes, the simple presence of a man can deter these would-be assaulters from their poisonous actions.

What a sick fucking world.

Jane put her head on my shoulder and whispered as Laura was walking down the hallway. "Matt, don't even worry about it. Laura didn't hear it, and I'm a big girl. It's not the first time, and unfortunately, it probably won't be the last time some jackass feels like he needs to say something. We've got tonight to focus on."

She gave me a kiss and walked into the kitchen, leaving me to stew in my thoughts.

When we pulled into the parking lot, Rich, Scarlett, and Sarah were already getting out of their car.

"You really don't think Sarah is going to be mad at me?" Laura said nervously from the backseat as she stared out the window toward her friend.

I turned in my seat to face her. "No, honey. I really don't think Sarah is going to be upset with you. You did the right thing."

A squeal of happiness came from outside and Sarah came running over to the car. Laura quickly unbuckled and opened her door just as Sarah got to it. The two friends hugged, and Sarah wished her a happy birthday before the car door shut once more. I looked at Jane and smiled, and she smiled back.

We got out and walked over to Rich and Scarlett, my hand extended to take Rich's. Jane's arms extended to pull Scarlett into an embrace. The girls stood under a flickering light outside the main entrance, watching the adults talk.

Even at a distance away, I could hear the buzzing of the light as it fought to shine down on the dark corner of the building. The back alley, where I imagined the dumpster and maybe even a homeless person or two fighting to stay warm would be. The brown brick building with its back facing the restaurant had no windows to help shine light in the dark. The alley was a darkened cave with unknown horrors.

The girls didn't notice. I did.

"What do you say we all get inside," I said, not taking my eyes off the darkened maw that stood behind the girls.

As we walked toward them, they opened the door with smiles on their faces. The smell of burgers wafted to us. Our mouths watered, the girls laughed as we made our way inside, and the streetlight flickered one last time.

Their laughter still hung in the air as darkness overwhelmed the parking lot.

Chapter 18

A loud rumble of thunder woke me from a deep sleep. My stomach was growling as the smell of cheeseburgers hung in the air. For a moment, I thought that perhaps it wasn't thunder but my churning guts that had woken me up. That thought was short-lived as another rumble shook the ground beneath the tent.

The blue hue of the tent darkened as rain began to pelt it with heavy, fat drops. I wondered if it was so dark because of the hour or the darkness of the sky. Perhaps both. I rolled over and saw Riley lying on her side, staring at me in a way that I thought showed sadness.

"Good morning," I said as I rubbed the sleep from my eyes.

"Good morning."

"It's nice to see you're actually inside the tent this time."

She gave me a soft smile and rolled onto her back. Her forehead creased with thoughts that seemed to be too heavy for one so young.

"You okay?" I asked quietly as I brought myself to a sitting position, my head resting against the back of the tent and feeling the soft massage of rain droplets rolling over the vinyl.

She sighed deeply, and I thought that maybe it was nothing more than the weather bringing her mood down.

The thunder rumbled again as I spoke. "Yeah, it's not going to be a fun walk today. Hopefully, it will clear up later."

"Hopefully," she said.

Feeling the urge to change the mood, I rose to my knees and said, "I'm going to go out and grab the last of the food. We'll have a nice breakfast and be on our way, okay?" I paused and rethought my words. "I don't suppose your friend left us any goodies again last night, did he?"

She shook her head slowly. "I don't think so. Not this time."

"Yeah, I was afraid of that. Well, we'll have some crackers and be on our way. I'll be right back."

"Sure," was all she managed. When I unzipped the flap, she spoke once more in a tone of quiet solemnity. "We're almost there."

I snapped my head back to look at her, a smile wide across my face. "Well, we better get moving then."

As I finally packed the sopping tent against my equally soaked backpack, I turned toward the forest and saw her there, looking off knowingly into the thicket of trees. It was very clear that something was weighing heavily on her mind. She should have been excited to be almost out, yet she was the opposite. Why would she not want to get home?

Then, another thought struck me. If she knew how to get out of the forest, why hadn't she left before?

I left my pack and walked toward her, unsure of what I would say when I approached. Always unsure of what to say in situations like this.

I caught myself fumbling with my shirt, pulling it down and smoothing out the wrinkles that weren't there as it clung to my skin.

"Everything okay?" I asked delicately.

The girl stood frozen. Her mind seemed to be a million miles away. Then she spoke, "I'm not ready for this to be over. I'm not sure you're ready either."

I chuckled. "Oh, believe me, I'm ready." I could see my attitude was doing nothing for hers. I put my hand on her shoulder. "Why aren't you happy? We'll be able to get you home to your family."

She turned to me with tears in her eyes. "You're the only family I know."

I pulled the girl close. True, we had only been in these woods together for a couple of days, but I felt an immense connection to her. Her bravery, her intelligence, her smile—it was infectious. I needed to get out of here, though I knew our journey would be over. But I suspected it would not be the last time I would see her. I'd keep in touch with her family, and watch her grow from afar. It made my heart happy to know that I was as important to her as she was to me.

I ruffled her hair. "Come on, kid. We're not out of here yet. Plus, damn this rain, I'm going to enjoy every last second we have together out here. You're my guide," I looked down at her face, pressed against my stomach, "and my friend."

The girl looked up at me and wiped away the tears that blended into the raindrops that dripped down the length of her face. She smiled, but when she looked behind me, her face changed to worry.

I turned around when I heard the snorts and panting of something large behind me. A large black bear was tearing through my pack, my father's pack. It had to have been brought in by the lingering smell of food that had coated the interior of the bag. My heart dropped and I felt my arm instinctually move the girl behind me. The bear had not seen us yet.

I watched as it ripped the red straps to shreds with its claws, its snout buried inside, unable to find the food that had left the scent upon it. I took a step back, pushing her slowly back into the forest, hoping to find shelter within the trees. However, when Riley's foot landed on a small branch, snapping it louder than I thought possible against the noise of the rainfall, the bear's head snapped out of the bag and stared directly at us.

"Don't move," I whispered sharply. I could feel her face in her hands, pressed up against my back. The bear took a step forward before rising up on its back legs. The immensity of the creature overwhelmed me. Clearly, this bear had been busy storing all the fat that it could before its long winter nap. Saliva dripped out of its mouth in long strings that hung almost to its chest. It let out a roar louder than the thunder that clapped simultaneously. My head swam with fear, and my legs buckled at the thought of being the bear's stand-in snack.

Suddenly, my father's voice rang out within me, and I had a vision of us sitting by a lake when I was a child. The lake was clear, and the day was perfect. It was autumn, and the leaves painted the landscape in yellows and oranges. The crisp smell of fall flooded my nostrils as I sat next to my old man, snacking on some crackers and listening to the silence of the forest. The moment was utter peace.

Across the lake, a bear strode out of the trees and stepped slowly into the cold water. I froze with fear though it was far enough away to not be a threat. My father looked over at me and laughed softly.

"You know, there is nothing to be afraid of."

I looked at him, anxiety growing within. I spoke as softly as I could, afraid the bear would hear my voice and come directly for us, tracking us until we were back in the car. "What do you mean nothing to worry about? It's *right there.*"

My dad looked back across the length of the lake and smiled. "Matt, that bear is not bothering us. He has no interest. He's interested in taking a bath and taking a drink. We'll be long gone before he gets over here."

I was unsure, but I knew I was safe with my dad. Though I knew I could trust him, I scooted away from the shoreline and stood up, wiping the dirt off my pants as I did so. "Still, I think it's time to go."

Dad looked back at the beauty of the lake and the large hill that it lay before and nodded. "You know, if you ever do run into a bear out in the wild, a black bear like that one at least, do you know what to do?"

I shook my head and pocketed the wrapper to the crackers that I had just finished off.

"Get big. Find a rock to stand on if you can, raise your arms over your head—show it you're bigger and badder than it is—and yell as loud as you can."

I thought he must be pulling my leg. "Really?"

He nodded and raised his arms above his head, and gave me the funniest angry face I had ever seen. I laughed, feeling a lot more confident now as my attention was taken off the bear. As we began to walk, a large orange leaf floated down from above and landed directly against my father's chest. He reached his hand up and grabbed it before it could fall to the ground and held it in front of himself.

"You know, Matt. The world can be a scary place. The woods, though, might be the least scary place to be." He turned the leaf over and ran his fingers against its edges. "But, you can't be scared all the time. Sometimes, you need to take a stand against the wrongs of the world. Sometimes, you need to fight your own fear and protect those you love. Because, as ugly as this world can be, there's a lot of beautiful things hidden in plain sight." He handed the leaf to me gently, almost as though he was afraid it would blow away and be lost with all the others. I took it and brought it to my nose, smelling the earthy scent. He bent over and picked up a yellow leaf that was much the same shape as the one I now held. "Now, I admit, sometimes the beauty of the world is really hard to find. But, sometimes, Matt, in order to find the hidden beauty, you just need to look beyond the autumn leaves."

I heard the girl whimper behind me as the bear took another step forward. My eyes searched the area and found, directly to my left, a large rock that sat about waist high. The perfect sitting rock. But, in this case, the perfect standing rock.

"Stay behind the rock," I told her. I felt her move to the side and saw the bear's eyes follow her. It let out another roar and brought itself back down on four legs.

My heart was racing, and were it not for the rain coming down in rivulets across my face, I fear the sweat would have stung my eyes. I took a deep breath and stood on the rock. The bear raised its head, following my eyes up. I could see in its eyes that it recognized now that I was much bigger than it had initially thought. Thunder boomed above us, and the bear rose once more to attempt and match my height. I raised my arms high above my head as the bear opened its mouth once more, its teeth yellow and sharp. It was then that I noticed the immensity of its claws. Butcher's knives coming out of fur. If this didn't work, I knew the girl and I were in a lot of trouble. I inhaled as deeply as I could and roared.

My throat tore, and somewhere in the recesses of my mind, I began to feel the emotion rise from within. All the sorrow I had felt from losing my dad built my scream into an explosion that startled the bear, freezing it where it stood. I saw confusion in its eyes as it lowered itself slowly back onto all four of its paws.

I had used up all the breath in my lungs but sucked in air one more time. The fear of falling from the cliff into the river, seeing the girl's *friend*, and seeing the beast that was most certainly not a friend. I felt the longing for my family, the agony they must be feeling when I didn't come home. My voice cracked as I once more felt my vocal cords straining against the pressure I was putting on them.

When I finally stopped my scream, tears were streaming from my eyes. The bear gave a hard shake of its head and turned away from us. It gave the backpack one last sniff and ran off into the woods in the opposite direction from which we were headed. I jumped down and sat on the rock, emotion overwhelming me. A shocked laugh escaped me and suddenly I couldn't catch my breath. I had just gone toe-to-toe with a bear and won. I couldn't believe I had that in me.

I felt a small hand against my back and was startled back to reality. The girl stood there, smiling ear-to-ear, staring at me with wonder in her eyes.

"Maybe I was wrong," she said. "Maybe you are ready." She wrapped her arms around my neck and pulled me close.

Chapter 19

The rain was incessant. Even with the canopy of the trees high above us, it came down in sheets. Fat globs fell off the colorful leaves that still clung to branches above our heads. Then, the rain would change altogether, and the wind would pick up and blow sharp, tiny drops across our exposed skin.

The tattered remnants of my bag hung off my shoulders, collecting rain and weighing it down against my weary body. The pack was beyond repair, but it was my father's pack, and I wasn't about to leave it. I had filled it back up with the remaining gear that I had and set forth, mentally preparing myself to retire the pack once I was home.

A chill ran through my bones as an owl hooted in the distance, clearly confused about the darkness of the forest when the sun should be shining through the trees. The temperature dropped the further we walked. What had started as a humid, warm day had changed into a cold, wet day. The worst kind of day. The kind of day that signaled something ominous just out of sight. The kind of day where you draw the shades and hunker down, afraid of what might come out of the dreary fog that was pressing down from above.

"Boy, this is one hell of a day," I said after about an hour of walking through the storm. "I hope it clears up soon."

"It won't," the girl said, her voice barely audible over the steady stream of rain slapping against the leaves above and below.

"Well, that's no way to think, Riley. The universe wouldn't allow for rain on what will be such a happy day. Once we get out of here, it's nothing but sunshine and rainbows." Even the rain couldn't keep my happiness at bay. Today was the day we'd be out of these damned woods, and though my anticipation was high, something was hiding in the depths of my mind. Some primal thing that signaled danger, yet I didn't heed its warning. Hell, maybe I didn't even truly recognize it was there.

"It always rains here. It's a place of sadness. But, it's a place we need to go to first."

"As long as we're going the right way."

We trod on, heads down and pushing forward. Making slow progress, but progress nonetheless.

When my boots landed on a soft part of the ground, water oozed up and covered the front. Not quite deep enough to go over the top, but close enough that I stopped and raised my head to see the girl several yards in front of me, stopped as well, looking off to her left.

In the distance, the trees opened up, and a dense fog clung to their trunks. It felt strange, unnatural. The fog looked as though someone had placed it there, hiding what wasn't meant to be seen.

"It's this way," the girl spoke somberly. "Watch your step. The ground isn't as solid as it looks in some places."

I raised my boot out of the water that was pooling deeper around it. "You can say that again."

As Riley stepped into the fog, she disappeared almost immediately. For the second time that day, I felt a sense of foreboding. There was something strange about these woods, yes. But there was something ominous about this place. I knew I was only a few feet behind her because as I walked, I could see her small footprints still being covered by the water that rushed over them.

"Hey, don't get too far ahead, okay? I can't see anything here."

The only response was the pattering of the rain against the leaves far above and the *slurp* of the ground with each step. A deep chill filled me, but whether that was from the fog or the feel, I was unsure.

"Hey, Riley. Don't go too far, okay?"

As I continued walking, thumbs hooked against the tattered red straps of my backpack, I realized her prints were no longer being covered over as I approached. In fact, there seemed to be no prints at all. I panicked.

"Riley?" My head snapped from left to right, but it was no use. The fog was too thick. I began forward again, but my feet became harder to lift against the suction of the muddy water. "Riley, where are you?"

Slurp, slurp. My legs strained against the pull of the earth. I could feel myself tiring quickly, and there was still no sign of Riley anywhere until I heard a soft voice in the distance.

"Matt…"

The fog was disorienting and I couldn't be sure what direction I had heard the voice from.

"Riley, where are you?"

"I don't know. But I'm stuck. I'm sinking."

My heart raced as I searched the all-encompassing gray world that I found myself in. Suddenly, I caught sight of lights to my right. Tiny flickers, momentary but clear against the dark world around me.

"Matt, help. It's up to my stomach. I can't move."

I moved my legs to a more solid position, recognizing that I was sinking slowly as well. In this other-worldly place, the only signal I saw was the flickering of the lights dancing. Dozens, maybe hundreds. I struggled forward as quickly as I could, hoping that Riley was in this direction because, I knew if she wasn't, she was lost.

And so was I.

I made slow progress toward the lights and suddenly realized they were moving in an orbital fashion around a giant tree—its roots massive and above the sinking earth beneath me. Riley screamed once more, and this time, I knew I was heading in the right direction.

"Just keep your arms out of the mud. Keep them up high. I'll find you."

"Matt, hurry. It's past my chest. I can't move."

I pulled myself up onto one of the protruding roots and searched. There she was, not five feet away from me, buried up to her neck, her arms frozen above her.

"Riley, I see you. Just hold on."

A guttural growl seemed to reverberate around us. My hair stood on end as I tried to decipher what animal could make such a noise while I searched for something to help Riley. A branch snapped above me and fell only inches from my head. I looked up to see where it came from and caught a glimpse of a greenish figure jumping away, high above the sucking swamp.

Another growl prompted me to grab the stick and stretch it as far as my arms would reach. "Grab the branch, Riley. You're almost there."

Her fingers fumbled with the branch as its end had become slick with muddy water. Another growl, this time significantly closer than before. My blood ran cold, but I stayed focused on Riley's grasping hands.

The muddy water was splashing into her mouth now. "Riley, grab the branch, and don't let go. DO NOT LET GO!"

"Matt…M-M," she struggled.

"HOLD YOUR BREATH." I reached with every last inch of my body, my shoulders straining, my muscles taut with effort. Just as her nose went under, she made one quick move forward, grasping the branch tightly before the shifting earth beneath dragged her under.

"RILEY!" I screamed into the gray world. But, before I could be swallowed up by the grief I was feeling, I felt a small tug against the branch that I still held—white-knuckled—in my grasp. The end of the branch was still beneath the mud. She had hold of it.

"Hold on, Riley. I've got you," I said, fighting all the doubt that my mind kept trying to throw in my path. I pulled hard. Steady, not jerking, I didn't want the branch to slip out of her grip, tenuous as it may be. My shoulders strained, and my teeth clenched as I pulled. The branch moved toward me, giving ground.

That same guttural growl echoed throughout the swamp, and somewhere in the distance, I thought I saw a shadow revealing itself—hovering above the quagmire.

The fireflies danced around me now, flickering and landing on me. With every pull, they illuminated brighter. Several flew away from me, hovering above where the branch was still buried, when her head appeared above the mud, and a gasp of fresh air filled her lungs.

"Riley! Oh, thank God. Just hold on. You're almost out."

I could see her eyes wide with fear and disorientation. But they showed something else, too. Resolve. I saw her little hands grip the branch tighter as I pulled harder. Her chest came out, and then her waist. When her feet were finally freed, I saw that her boots had been lost. Buried for eternity in this strange place.

When she was close enough, I reached forward and grabbed her, dragging her out of the mud and into my lap, wiping her mouth and hair. Her body rested against me, her breath deep and ragged. I figured she must have swallowed at least some of the mud. I could only hope not too much.

I pressed her against me and squeezed tightly. "You're okay now. You're okay."

"Th…thank you," she breathed softly into my chest.

I bent down and kissed the top of her head and then froze as I let my eyes wander past the tree. The blood drained from my face, and my stomach sank into the pit of oblivion. Riley could feel my body tense, and without looking up, she spoke again.

"What's wrong?"

There, roughly ten feet from where we sat, though still shrouded in darkness and fog, was the silhouette of something awful. Its hulking mass hung several feet above the soft ground as its leathery wings flapped slowly, not moving forward but hovering. I could make out no physical features save the wings, but its guttural growl, low and brewing, kept all my nerve endings at attention.

"Just don't move, Riley. Keep your head against my chest. It'll be alright."

I felt her face pull only inches away from me, and her eyes looked up to mine. "It's here, isn't it?"

I nodded slowly. "Just stay still."

"It has been after me since I got here. Now it's got both of us." She cried softly against me as she rested her head back on my chest, exhaustion threatening to fully take over.

The growl grew to a deep rumbling that I could feel reverberate through me. As it slowly flapped its awful wings, it got closer. My bones were rattling; my breath was shaky as though it had to push past the lump in my throat. I felt Riley's mouth moving against me, and I was surprised to see her mouthing words that I could not hear. *Prayer*, I thought. *Maybe I should find God, too.*

The world moved in slow motion as the beast hung above me. Now I could see its features, though I wished it was still hidden in the gray world in front of me. Its eyes were dark red and serpentine. Its chest rippled with muscles that gleaned behind sweat-covered flesh. Its legs were covered with hair, and though it wore no clothes, there were no sex organs to speak of. Its feet were cloven and monstrous. My eyes traveled slowly back up its body as gooseflesh broke out all over me.

The beast's wings continued to flap, pushing cool, humid air against my face. The stench coming off of the being's body was putrid—sulfur and decay together. It made my stomach turn as I reeled against it. When it leaned forward and sniffed the air around us, I caught a momentary whiff of its breath, and bile threatened to spill from my lips.

The beast looked down at me, sitting on the roots with Riley curled up in my lap—sobbing quietly—and sneered.

Then it spoke.

"You do not belong here."

I couldn't take my eyes off the demonic thing hovering above me. Somewhere in the recesses of my mind, I registered a bit of what was said, but it didn't make sense as a complete sentence. The fireflies continued to hover around us, but a stray light would occasionally get too close to the monster, and I'd watch its light fade as it fell onto the soggy earth.

The beast leaned closer. **"You do NOT belong here. Why have you come?"**

Nothing made sense. This beast, it *couldn't* be here. And, if it was truly here, it *couldn't* speak to me in any sort of language I could understand. *So why can I?*

As my tongue wet my lips, allowing myself another moment to process what I was seeing and hearing, my throat clenched and relaxed, trying to find the response that would satisfy the beast. The problem was I didn't understand the question.

"I-I…" I felt Riley's mouth still moving in silent prayer when I saw another shadow high above. This shadow was slimmer, still built wide, but less so than the hulking beast before us. It appeared to be jumping from branch to branch in leaps far too wide for any forest creature that I could think of in the northeast. It moved meticulously. It moved gracefully. It moved with purpose.

The beast's head moved slightly to its right as it sniffed the air. That's when I felt the weight against me lessen as Riley rose and stood defiantly before the hateful thing.

"Hey!" she yelled, her voice giving off a power that I hadn't heard before. "Why don't you just get out of here!"

The beast's eyes left mine, and my mind began to clear. The beast flapped its wings forward and lowered itself to mere inches off the soggy earth as it leaned forward to take in the little girl before it. The rumbling growl began in its throat again, and while I found myself frozen in place, Riley stood her ground.

"You don't scare me, you know? When I first saw you, you did. But not now. I'm not going with you, so just get away from me."

"Oh, young one. How wrong you are." The beast slowly reached its clawed hand out to place upon her head. Though she stood in front of me, I could sense her eyes following the slow movement of its hand. Just as the beast was about to grab her hair, she reached her hand up and slapped it away.

"I said GO!" she screamed.

"Wretched, BITCH!" the beast hissed, bringing its arm far above Riley. **"You have been here too long. You are MINE."**

Its arm came down fast, appearing faster still as it crossed in front of the slow yet powerful flapping of its wings.

I found myself broken out of the haze that had overtaken me. I screamed at the beast and reached my arms out to grab Riley's shirt. I felt my fingers close around the fabric as the beast's arm was about to strike.

Suddenly, the shadow was back. This time, not high above, but closing the distance between the branch that had kept it hidden above only moments before and the hulking arm that was coming down upon the girl. I pulled Riley back into my lap as the arm sliced down. I felt the force of the attack when the arm went slicing just in front of her nose.

Milliseconds later, the beast was face down, sinking into the earth while the green and wooden being that Riley had called her friend pressed its head further into the muddy ground. The beast's wings flapped forcefully, but her friend had placed its knee (if what this being had could indeed be called knees) into the middle of the beast's back.

It kept its hand tightly against the evil one's head as it sank lower. When the last sign of its wings was sunken below the grassy top layer, Riley's friend released its grip and jumped with mighty legs out of the mud and onto a root next to us.

The mud gurgled as the top layer closed in over the spot where the wicked beast was buried. Riley leaped from my lap and jumped over to where the large being made of earth and wood stood. She wrapped her arms around its leg and pushed her face into the grass patch that would be its stomach if it had what we know as a stomach.

For the first time, I got to take in this being. It was strikingly calming to be so close to it. Its aura extended from where it stood to where I sat feet away. It was as though being near it…warmed me. For the first time in days, I felt the welcoming feeling of sitting by a fire on a cold, snowy night; the feeling of wrapping yourself up in a blanket—fresh out of the dryer—and listening to the sounds of thunder roll over the mountains as you dive into a good book; the feeling of being home.

The being took its eyes off of Riley and looked at me. It was hard to make out any features on it other than, that is, its eyes. They say that the eyes are the gateway to the soul. The eyes I looked into at that moment spoke a lifetime of words in fleeting seconds. It looked at me with sympathy and with caring. It looked at me with longing and sadness. It looked at me with knowing.

And then it looked away from me, and its eyes widened in fear.

I looked down between the roots that I was sitting on, and I could see the layer of grass over the muddy depths below. Water was bubbling up over the top layer as the semi-fluid earth shook against the force of wings beating against it. I could hear the *slurping* noise as the mud tried desperately to hold on to its prey. A battle that the prey, this time, would win.

I turned my head slowly, away from Riley and her friend, and my heart sank as the beast rose out of its muddy grave, eyes lowered and staring hatefully at the being that had dared stand in its way once more. Its growl was more fierce than it had been. As its mouth steadily opened, the growl turned to a scream. A scream that sounded like the deepest depths of the underworld where the souls of the damned are tortured in perpetuity.

I raised my hands to my ears and lowered my head to my chest. I thought my body would burst from the pressure that filled the air in the wake of that awful sound. I felt Riley at my back once more, her forehead pressing against me; her hands, I had to assume, covering her ears also.

When the screaming slowly died out, my head was left ringing. I could feel warm tears running down my cheeks, though I felt no pain. I felt nothing. My body was numb, as though the reverberations in the air around me, first from the growling and next from the scream, had set all my nerves into overdrive, shorting them out.

I allowed myself to look up, not sure I wanted to see what was in front of me, but determined that if I was going to meet my maker, I'd do it as fearlessly as I could. The beast was there, mere feet away, hovering once more above the earth. Its muscles stood taut against its flesh. It was a terrifying sight to see as the mud dripped from its face and down its heaving chest. But, it paid me no mind.

I followed its unholy eyes and found that it stared directly at the one that had saved us. Riley's friend stood at its full height and with its chest pushed out, showing no fear in the eyes of death. I sat dumbstruck, too afraid to move and be seen. We were too vulnerable to attack. The being took its eyes off of the beast and looked at Riley. It pointed just beyond the tree and nodded its head. Once again, I saw sadness. Whatever this being was, it knew things that I'll never know. It wasn't from here, yet nothing felt so natural as being in its aura.

It turned its eyes to me, and they morphed into something different: resolve. The same resolve that I had seen in Riley's eyes, scared as she was when I was pulling her from the mud. Yes, this entity had been her friend, and it had taught her well. It slammed its wooden fist into its chest and brought its attention back entirely to the heinous thing in front of it.

The evil thing roared and, with one hard flap of its wings, came crashing into Riley's friend, slamming it against the massive tree trunk and scattering the remaining fireflies that had stuck around to show their support.

"No!" Riley screamed as her friend was pinned down only feet from us. The evil being crushed her friend's head into the trunk, splintering it with force, and looked back at Riley.

"I told you, you're mine!"

Riley shrunk against my back only moments before a mighty wooden fist cracked against the beast's chin, causing it to fall to the side of the wounded being. Wood splintered at the top of its head. At that moment, its eyes didn't show sadness or resolve but stunned confusion. It raised its hand once more and pointed in the same direction as before. I looked to where it was pointing and saw the thick trees spread as they had before the moose attack, and the ground appeared to firm itself. I looked back to the crumpled body of the being that had kept Riley safe for an unknown amount of time and smiled.

The evil being shook its head as it righted itself with the power of its wings. When it turned its head, my stomach rolled once more. Its jaw hung at an awful angle, clearly dislocated from the force of the blow it had taken. The beast took one of its massive clawed hands and grabbed the hanging bone. With a sharp push up and in, I heard the snapping of bone against bone as the joint found its correct socket.

"We've got to go, Riley."

"No," she whimpered. "No, it wants me. It's going to kill him, but it wants me."

Her friend turned once more and motioned its head to the path that had formed for us. I stood and grabbed Riley in one fluid motion and held her tight. She struggled against me for only a moment before resigning herself to our escape and letting her head rest against my shoulder.

The monster growled again, and I turned to see it pressing its full weight down upon her friend while glaring at us. I heard the cracking of wood underneath its massive foot, and I covered Riley's eyes with my free hand. My foot slipped off the root, and I stumbled backward, catching myself only as my back hit the trunk of the tree. When I looked back, the monster was standing directly at my side.

"You will go nowhere. You do not belong here, but here you will stay."

I turned to run and stepped onto ground that was as firm as the trail we had walked on for days. Behind us, there was a terrible crash and the sound of wood snapping. I was horrified to think that it was her friend's body breaking in such a way, but when I heard the sound of an entire tree coming down beside us, I turned and looked back.

Next to the broken body of the wooden being that had saved us was a full-fledged battle. The evil beast was rising from the moss-covered roots, and beings that looked like Riley's friend swung down from branches high above or leaped from roots out of the attacking range of the monster.

They seemed to come from every direction, though I was sure there couldn't have been more than three or four of them. They struck, faded into the fog or up into the trees, and repeated. Just as the trees closed in around us I heard a massive roar and turned to see the beast, with one hard, fast motion of its wings, fly high into the sky.

I ran as fast as I could for as long as I could. I ran until Riley asked me to stop.

I ran until she told me that we had made it.

We were there.

She glided out of my arms and onto the solid ground. My body felt as though it were floating after the run through the forest, my heart yet to catch up with the rest of my body. I looked around, utterly confused.

"Riley, where are we?" I asked as I turned in a full circle, taking in my surroundings. The trees that had opened up to allow us somewhere to flee had now once again closed around us. Trunks, virtually impossible to pass by, closed in on us from all sides. Above, autumn leaves fell upon us in a rainbow.

The silence of this place left a buzzing in my ears that I wasn't entirely positive didn't come from the scream of the beast that we had seemingly escaped. No squirrels running through downed leaves. No birds calling out a warning that humans were amongst them. Silence held this place tight, unwilling or unable to loosen its grip.

Riley faced away from me, her shoulders slowly rising up and down with each breath, her heart racing still from our escape. She faced the direction we had been running, staring at the mouth of a massive cave cut out of a sheer rock wall. I let my eyes follow the wall as high as I could see. For a fleeting, fearful moment, I remembered the cliff yesterday that she insisted we climb down to the river. There was no way she was insisting we go up this.

"Riley, there is no way we are going up there," I said finally.

"No, we're not."

"So then, where the hell are we? You said we were here." My frustration began to build as my desperation to leave these woods took over.

She turned slowly and stared at me. Tears rolled over the dimples on her face. My heart broke to see her sad again.

"Do you know me?" she asked curiously.

I shook my head, unsure I heard her correctly. "Do I know you?"

She stepped close to me, and I kneeled down to face her directly. "Yes, do you know me?"

"I-I don't understand."

"Riley…I know you've been thinking about my name since I told it to you."

She was right. I had been. It was just a name, sure. But why did it hit my heart the way it did?

"Matt…this place isn't like other places."

I let out a soft laugh. "You can say that again."

"No, I mean…"

"What?"

She spoke slowly, deliberately to me, annunciating every syllable. "Riley. You remember me, don't you?"

My head began to swim as thoughts that I had dared not entertain, crazy thoughts, entered my mind.

"Dad," she whispered. "Remember." She placed her soft hands on the sides of my head.

I gasped, and my body shook. Suddenly, I was laying on my back amongst the autumn leaves, in darkness.

Chapter 20

I was abruptly back at my house, on the deck with Jane, sitting in front of breakfast and taking in the warm morning breeze. I could hear the birds chirping and the breeze whispering in my ear as it blew past me. It felt so real.

I remembered that morning, that awful morning. But it wasn't awful yet. In this moment, life was still happy, still beautiful. I heard my wife's voice as though she were standing right next to me.

"Matt, we need to decide on names. A boy name and a girl name."

"Maybe a name that could be either sex. That way, we don't need to worry about whether we're having a boy or a girl. We'll have a name either way."

She smiled at me as she took a mouthful of my homemade French toast. "You're always looking for the easy way out." She snickered.

"Work smarter, not harder."

She took a big gulp of her chocolate milk and swallowed down the last of the French toast still in her mouth. "No, you're right though. I like that idea."

"See, you're with a very smart man."

Jane leaned over and gave me a playful whack on the arm. "Don't let your head get too big."

I had shoveled some eggs in my mouth and sat back in my chair. "How about…" My mind searched for a gender-neutral name. "How about Peyton, or Morgan, or—"

"Riley," she said. At that moment, it all felt as though it had clicked into place. Riley was the perfect name. The perfect name for our perfect unborn child.

I leaned forward, kissed her, and stared into her eyes. "Riley. That's perfect."

Jane finished her glass of milk and sat back. A glow still covering her face. Happiness still swelling inside her.

"Jane, oh God. Are you okay?"

"What do you mean?" she asked, seemingly unaware.

"You're bleeding. Are you—"

At that moment, she screamed and bent completely forward in her seat. My heart sank again, as it had the day this all happened the first time.

Jane, the deck, and the warm breeze all faded away in an instant, and I felt myself being sucked back into time, further than before. My mind raced, and though I knew I was unconscious, I could feel my stomach rolling with the obscure passage of time.

When my vision had stopped spinning, I found myself on a familiar trail, standing beneath a set of ladders that led to the summits of the mountains I had been on as a kid. Again, my stomach rolled at the fear of the unknown that lay in front of me. *What if I fall? What if I **DIE**?*

"What's wrong?" My dad's voice hit me like a ton of bricks. Even in this confused state, all my emotions were able to be tapped into, and hearing my father's voice, clear as day, after so long, sent a shockwave of pain throughout my body.

"Dad, there is no way that I can climb those. The map shows a trail just over there. We can skip this part."

"Nonsense," I heard him say in his typical jovial way. "This will be a piece of cake."

"Dad, I really don't know…"

"Tell you what, why don't you watch me first and see how easy it is."

I had thought about this momentarily and nodded, comfortable at the bottom of this climb. Dad climbed the ladders with ease and turned to face me when he got to the top. He let out a scream of accomplishment and motioned for me to follow him up.

I could feel the wooden rung under my hands all over again. The feel of my boot gripping the rung below me as I willed myself to climb slowly, carefully. I thought how silly it was to be as afraid of the ladders as I had been. Then, I found myself needing to cross over the small gap and grab hold of the third ladder just below where my father stood.

I looked down, and the world below me started to spin. I hugged the ladder tightly, suddenly too afraid to move.

"Matt, you're okay," I heard from above. "You're doing great so far. You're almost there."

I could feel my palms getting sweaty, giving the illusion that my grip was slipping and I would soon fall, leaving me mangled and likely dead among the rocks below. "Dad, I'm stuck. I can't move."

"Yes, you can, Matt. Just take it slow." He saw me readjust my grip on the ladder and spoke the words that would convince me to push myself outside my comfort zone. "Every day we take risks in life, Matt. You just have to calculate them and take the safest way around them or over them. Don't let fear rule you. Look at your situation and find the solution."

I opened my eyes and looked at the ladder. It still seemed so far away. Then I looked just to my right, just next to the bottom rung of the third ladder, and saw a rock jutting out, wide enough for me to get my entire boot on it and still grasp the ladder I was on.

I slowly raised my right foot and placed it on the ledge, still gripping the ladder with both hands. Once my foot was steady, I raised my left foot to the top of the ladder, giving myself a solid base to let go with my right hand and stretch to the third ladder. I grabbed it and, for only a moment, froze again.

"That's right, Matt. You're almost there."

I let go of the ladder with my left hand and placed it just above me on a small hold that was sticking out of the wall. Then, all in one motion, I pulled myself up, allowing my right leg to reach for the bottom rung of the third ladder and my left foot to find the same rock that my right foot had just vacated. Finally, I pulled myself up to the second rung and brought my left foot over. I had done it.

My father let out another scream of accomplishment, and once I was off the ladder, he pulled me to him and hugged me tightly. I looked down at the drop I had just ascended and felt a sense of accomplishment wash over me. Pride swelled within me.

"See, you can do anything you want. Just look at your situation and find the best way to overcome it. Don't let fear rule the day."

Dad disappeared in a sudden poof of smoke, and the world spun around me once more. I could hear voices in the distance. Voices that I recognized but couldn't put my finger on. Reds and whites flashed before my eyes as my spinning mind began to slow.

"…so that's what we have to do, Rich, Scarlett. We'll go down to the school tomorrow morning with you. We'll find out what is going on once and for all, and if we need to, we'll go to the police station with you immediately after," Jane said from her stool across from Sarah's parents.

My head felt woozy, but I recognized the inside of *Yummy Burger* easily. The savory smell of cheeseburgers filled my nostrils, and my mouth began to water with the anticipation of a full belly of red meat.

The bells and whistles of *Yummy Burger's* arcade caught my attention, and I saw Laura and Sarah laughing as a boy a little older than them took and missed almost every shot in one of those basketball shooting games where the rim moves. It was lovely to see them smiling together, momentarily forgetting the trauma they had experienced.

"We'll all be okay once this pervert is out of the area and locked behind bars. I still can't believe the school didn't tell us. That they tried to sweep it under the rug." Jane was on the verge of tears, and I placed a hand against her back.

"Dad, can we have a few more dollars for tokens?" Sarah asked as she gleefully ran up to the table.

"Sorry, honey. We have to get going soon. It's a school night," Rich said despite the forlorn look on the girls' faces.

"Yeah, we need to think about going too, Laura."

Rich and Scarlett stood up and grabbed their jackets while the two girls hugged each other and said they'd catch up tomorrow in class. Scarlett and Rich said their goodbyes with promises to meet at the school before it got out tomorrow afternoon.

"Dad, I have a few more tokens. Can I use them before we leave?" I never could say no to Laura, at least not easily, so I gave in.

"Sure, but hurry up, okay? It's getting late."

For the next fifteen minutes, Jane and I stood by Laura, watching her roll the skeeball up the track and counting the few tickets that came spitting out below her. When the last of her tokens had run out, she smiled at us and said she was going to save the tickets for next time. Maybe even split them with Sarah, in case she got sad again.

I handed Jane the keys, and the girls left *Yummy Burger* first; I had to stop at the bathroom before our trip home. When I stepped outside, only a few minutes later, I was overwhelmed by the darkness of the parking lot. The clouds above hid the moon, allowing for the shadows of evil things to lurk in the black void of the lot and beyond. No cars drove by. Snow fell lightly around us, dampening the honks of horns far in the distance. A chill ran up my spine as a feeling of dread washed over me.

The car was still off, a corpse in the wicked night. I took a few steps closer, thinking I must be wrong and that they had simply not turned on the lights when I heard a muffled cry from the back corner of the building.

"Honey?" I called into the darkness. When I heard the shrill scream of Laura's voice, my blood ran cold.

"Dad, help!"

I leaped over the small snow mound that slightly blocked the alley at the back of *Yummy Burger*. I hardly noticed the three sets of footprints, one much smaller than the others, one much larger. My senses heightened. The smell of cheeseburgers attacked my nostrils, the thunderclap of each flake of snow striking the pavement, the shadow of a man pressing a woman against the brick building, a smaller one with her arms wrapped around her legs, hidden in the corner.

"Matt, he's got a gun." Then she said to the man, pressing his arm into her back, "Please, please don't hurt us."

As my eyes adjusted to the dark, I recognized a dark hooded sweatshirt. At first, I thought he was wearing those gloves with the missing fingertips, but then I realized that each finger had a tattoo on it. My mind flashed to the man I saw only momentarily in front of Laura's school. The same man that was outside of our house at her birthday party. The same evil being who had traumatized Sarah and was after Laura.

I held my arm up in front of me and took a slow step forward. "Listen to me, let them go. Do you understand? Let them go and disappear into the night or so help me…"

The flash of light was so sudden and blinding that I thought someone, somewhere, must have turned on a flashlight and shone it at my face. I shielded my eyes but found myself bent over at the waist, warmth running down my leg.

I was confused, and then, as if on tape delay, I heard the loud *pop* of a gun and the louder screams of my wife and daughter. I felt my legs give out, and I landed on the pavement. My back was bitterly cold, the open hole in my stomach spewing out warmth.

My lips moved as if asking a silent question to the universe. The cold of the pavement on won the night as I began to feel the warmth drain out of me from toe to head. My eyes drifted to the sky as the clouds opened up, and the moon shone down on me from above.

My eyes were heavy.

So heavy.

When they closed, I was comforted by the darkness that held me in its grasp.

Jesus, how long have I been driving?

The world was spinning faster now. My mind became more chaotic as I tried to understand what was happening to me. I saw myself climbing the Alpine Staircase. I saw myself on the summit of Mount Whitehorse, whispering words to my father, who I knew was watching me from somewhere. I saw my father's bag a distance away from the sitting rock that I had left it by.

Then, I saw my father. "Matt…" he said as he reached out to me before I fell into the bitterly cold water. I could feel the water taking me, rushing me downriver. I could smell the mud as I crawled out of the water.

My mind rushed forward once more, and I saw her.

Riley.

Our daughter.

Our miscarried daughter.

Chapter 21

My eyes opened, and the fogginess of my brain broke apart like clouds after a storm. I blinked away the blurriness and found myself staring up at a blue sky. My eyes caught a single red leaf high above me, shaking in the light breeze. I watched it tear away from the branch and slowly glide down, spinning end-over-end before landing on my chest. It rose and fell with each slow exhalation, but suddenly, I felt myself energized by fear.

Where is Riley?

I sat up with a start and felt the rough, papery leaf slide down my shirt. My hands dug into the dirt, somehow drier than I expected after all the rain. *How long had I been out?*

I clenched the dirt into my fists, frustrated at myself for losing her. Frustrated that I had blacked out. Terrified at what I had discovered.

I was dead. Or, at least, dying. I was somewhere not on Earth—at least, not Earth in the way I knew it. As I sat there, it all seemed to come together. All the strange happenings that I had seen over the last few days. The woods opening and closing as they seemed to please. Riley's friend. The evil being that stalked us.

"And what about me?"

I leaped up from my spot in the dirt and stifled a scream. "Dad?"

I turned and saw my father standing only feet behind me. He was wearing his typical red flannel shirt and jeans. His hair hadn't grayed at all in the time that he'd been gone. His smile shone brighter than the warm sun above. He looked exactly as I remembered.

"H-How are you…"

"This place," he started, "it's wonderful, isn't it?"

I looked over my shoulder in the direction he was staring. The mouth of the massive cave beckoned to me. The blackness of it against the now-clear sky made my stomach drop.

"Dad, I-I don't know." He took his eyes away from the cave and looked at me. "I just want to go home. I want to go home to my family."

He smiled and took a step closer to me. He reached out a hand and placed it on my shoulder—the same comforting gesture he offered when I was young. "Well, Matt, I'm afraid that can't happen right now."

"What do you mean?" I stepped away from him and ran my fingers through my hair, trying to get a sense of clarity. "Those memories… were they real?"

"I'm afraid so, son."

"So…so, I'm dead?"

He lowered his eyes and, once more, took a step closer to me. "No, not dead. Dying, I suppose." He smiled again. "But you see, death is not the end. We have this place."

"But, we were never religious. Are you telling me this is heaven?"

My father shook his head sharply. "No, not heaven. I've heard it called 'limbo' or 'purgatory,' but this place can't be chiseled down to a singular word."

My head swam, and my legs threatened to give out. "Why am I here?"

"We all come here. Well, our energy, at least. You see, Matt, I don't know if we all have souls. Souls, to me, are a religious concept. But we all have energy. And that's what you are now. Energy."

"So, my body…"

"In the alley behind that restaurant you took Laura to. Laying in the snow, getting colder by the second."

My mind flashed to the memory of Jane being pushed up against the exterior of the building behind the restaurant. Laura, scared and cold, curled up in the darkness with her head between her knees. I was wasting time.

"Oh, God, Dad, I need to get back. There is this guy, this terrible guy, he's hurting Jane. He's hurting Laura."

He rested his hand on my shoulder again and looked me in the eyes. "Don't worry about them. At least, not yet. Time runs differently here. Our energies respond differently than our bodies do to the passing of time."

"What do you mean?" I asked with panic in my voice.

"You've been here for three days. But your body was only shot seconds ago."

"You mean…"

"Yes, they are still there. Still mourning your seemingly deceased body. They cry out for you still, but you must make a choice first."

There was movement in the woods behind my father. Movement that made my heart skip, yet my father didn't move. His eyes remained focused on me. Suddenly, several of the beings that Riley had called *friends* came out from behind the trees. They were not crying, but their heads were held low, and their eyes held a painful sorrow that I could only imagine my wife and daughter felt at the same time—in a different place.

Two of the bigger beings carried the fallen body of the one that had helped Laura survive. Its limp, broken body looked awkward being carried in such a way. What had once appeared so strong, now looking so weak. There was a soft moaning from the group as they walked by my father and me, not giving a glance in our direction. The moaning gave me a strong sense of loss, but it wasn't absolute. It was as though they were giving their friend a "goodbye for now" but not a final farewell.

I turned and watched them as they made their way up the small incline and toward the mouth of the cave, the soft moaning becoming a distant feeling rather than an auditory noise. The sound disappeared entirely as the beings walked into the darkness of the cave and disappeared.

"Are you ready to make your choice?" My father's voice startled me from my trance-like state.

"What's the choice?"

"It is a difficult one. One that I've seen others have to make, but this is the first time I've had to direct someone to make it."

"Tell me, Dad."

"You must decide to go into the cave, the underworld, and find Riley, save her, learn from this place, and return to your body…"

"Or…?"

"Or, you stay with me."

A weight fell upon my heart as I thought about the consequences of either choice. The warmth that surrounded me now in this place being with my father again, pulled at me. It called to me like sirens calling to Odysseus and his men. I fell to my knees and looked to the sky once more, searching for answers to questions with impossible choices.

"If I stay, will we be with Riley?"

My father shook his head and knelt in front of me. "No. Riley has been taken by the beast. When she placed her hands on your temples, just after you collapsed, it took her. It took her deep within the cave.

"If you stay with me, we will go to the next place. We will go together, and we'll no longer be in this place or where your body is. She will be lost, but your energy will remain. Jane and Laura will survive, though they will experience things that no energy should have to experience."

"But if I go, I'll lose you…again. I don't know if I can do that. Not again."

Dad smiled, and he helped me up so that I was standing in front of him. "True, you will leave this place without me. You will go back to your body. But you won't lose me forever, just for a time. I'll be here when your time arrives again."

A soft cry echoed inside my head. A cry from another place, calling out to me from a darkened alley in another world. I knew I needed to get back to them. But there was no way I could just leave Riley to that beast. I needed to save her before I could save them.

Comfort swelled within me as I felt more confident in my decision. Knowing he would not be lost to me forever, knowing our energies would meet again, gave me strength.

I rushed forward and wrapped my arms around him. I held him close and felt his breath against my neck. Even in death, he was able to guide me, to teach me what was right. "Thank you, Dad."

"You're welcome, Matthew."

"I miss you every single day."

"And I, you. But remember, your body's death is not the end. When your time comes, I'll be there."

I released my grip on him, and he grabbed my face, holding my gaze to his. A look of seriousness overcame him. A look I had never seen before. I had seen him be serious many times, but that expression was always touched with determination, guts, will. This look was clouded with fear.

"Matt, go to her. Save Riley's energy, and she will be safe with me. But, whatever you do, don't let the beast take you. You will be in its domain. If your energy is destroyed while you're in there…you will be lost."

I stepped back, suddenly fearful of my choice. I hated taking risks, and this was the biggest one imaginable. "But, if that's true, then Riley is already lost."

A fearful look turned back into grim determination. "No, it keeps her at the cusp of its domain. It is using her as bait. It wants you now. Your energy is fresh, new. It knows you'll come for her."

I lowered my head, unsure of my decision. "Dad, I—"

"Matthew, you have always given me pure joy. From the moment I first held you, I knew that I could never be happier, and I never was. I tried to teach you, to guide you, to get you to trust yourself. Trust in all you have inside you. We all need to take risks in life sometimes, Matt. You just need to look at your situation and find the best way to overcome it. Don't let fear rule the day. You're making the right choice."

The memory of the ladders flooded back with his words. I lunged forward again and pulled him close, this time unsure if I was willing to ever let go. The colorful leaves began to fall all around us as we embraced. The calmness of the woods allowed me to hear each fall on top of those that already had.

"This place is wonderful, isn't it?" he asked again.

I stepped back, picked up a dark red leaf, and held it in front of my eyes, then turned to the cave. "There is a lot of beauty here." I held the leaf close to my eyes, blotting out the gaping maw of the cave that stood before me. "You just need to look beyond the autumn leaves."

Though my back was turned, I could hear the smile on my dad's face as he spoke. "Be safe, son. I love you."

"I love you, too, Dad."

I took my first step toward the cave.

Toward the darkness.

To save her.

Chapter 22

The heavy, damp air draped across my body the moment I stepped foot into the mouth of the cave. The temperature dropped with my confidence as I stepped further into the darkness, saying goodbye to the light that, at least, my mind had convinced me at that moment, was safety. My hearing slowly became attuned to the quiet of the cave, and I found myself marveling at how the little rivulets of water that streamed down the cave walls sounded like tiny waterfalls shaping the cave millimeters at a time.

My vision slowly adapted to the darkness, and I began to notice the contours of the cavern. Shimmering flecks of quartz danced in front of me as I took small steps forward. Unwilling to fully trust my eyes yet, I let my fingertips brush against the slick, rough walls that surrounded me. I jumped back in horror when I felt my fingers push up against a semi-solid ball of what I can only describe as snot. I rubbed my hand against my pants, desperate to get the goo off my fingers. When my terror subsided with the slowing of my heartbeat, I realized it had been no more than a slug slowly making its way up the wall and toward a crack several feet above where it currently sat.

I was still close to the entrance, close enough that I did not want to turn around and let the daylight blind me, so I kept going forward, even though every muscle in my body begged me to turn around and run. When I found myself standing at a dead end, I didn't know what to do. I searched the wall from the top down when my heart hit the floor. I noticed a crawl space, not much taller than I'd be lying on my stomach, at my feet.

There's no way, I thought, *no fucking way*.

I crouched down to get a better look and was horrified to see thick webs covering the hole. A few large, dark-colored spiders crawled into the corners as they recognized that I was looking in their direction. My stomach turned, and gooseflesh covered me from head to toe.

No fucking way.

I stood up and let my eyes scan the wall in front of me again. There *had* to be another way. I figured I'd probably fit if I left my backpack, my dad's backpack, behind, but the webs weren't even broken. There was just no way Riley had gone through there, let alone a being the size of the beast that had taken her. But there had to be a way around. In fact, where were the beings that had watched over Riley? I had watched them enter only a few minutes before I did, and they were nowhere to be found.

"Damnit," I called out as I kicked the wall. "What am I supposed to do?"

Look at your situation and find the solution. My dad's voice echoed in my head. A quiet, low rumble came from behind the wall I was standing in front of. There was something back there. That had to be the way. I knelt down once again, looking at the small crawl space with the spiders hiding in the corners of their webs, and gathered my composure. I stripped off my pack and let it rest up against the wall, making a mental note to come back for it at all costs. Some strange afterlife world or not, that pack was not going to be left there.

When I lay down, my heart began to race. I had thoughts of spiders crawling over my back, my face, in my shirt, but the worst thought of all was simply…what if I got stuck? The fear of not being able to take a deep breath, of feeling unknown tons of earth and rock crushing down on my body, made me sick to my stomach. I tried to calm myself with slow, deep breaths. In through the nose, out through the mouth.

As I was about to clear the first web from in front of me, something crawled over my legs. I let out a shrill scream of one who just had death walk over him, although this wasn't death— this was a little rodent. *A vole*, I thought they were called.

I watched the little creature move off to my left, deeper into the darkness. I followed it until it was no more than a shadow, darker than the darkness that hid the corner of the cave when suddenly, it was gone. I stood up, and brushed myself off, a futile and reactionary effort to clean my ruined pants, when I realized how foolish I had been. I reached down into the pack and pulled out the headlamp I had stored within.

I clicked the button to turn it on, and the cave was illuminated fully. I noticed the wall that the vole had gone near seemed to curve around the backside. I ran to the corner and realized that there was a narrow path around the backside of the wall. Narrow, yes, but not nearly as narrow as the crawlspace I almost found myself sharing with the spiders. I pressed through the passage, my shoulders touching both sides of the wall, and found myself in a large open room that rose dozens of feet in the air.

"What is this place?"

"Dad, help me!" Riley's voice cut through the darkness beyond my light like a flare through the night, guiding me.

"Riley!" I shouted and picked up speed as I moved toward her voice. Even with the headlamp lighting the way, I hesitated to run at full speed, knowing if I took one wrong step here, Riley would be lost; I would be, too.

The end of the room had two distinct pathways going in two opposite directions. To my left, more spiderwebs, more darkness, more feelings of dread washing over me. To my right, a path illuminated by the dullest of lights somewhere far in the distance, the sound of water falling obscuring the otherwise total silence that now surrounded me.

The dark beast that had taken Riley seemed to be laughing at me, challenging me to make the right decision yet making me second-guess everything. I looked down the ominous tunnel to the left and froze, sure something as evil as this beast had taken her down there. I stepped forward and suddenly had a vision clear in my mind. A vision of Riley and I in the pool of water by the falls.

She's down there!

I turned to the right tunnel and ran forward as fast as I dared. The sound of the water got louder with each step until, suddenly, I found myself in another room, this one taller than the last. A waterfall, beautiful and blue, rose a hundred feet in the air. Above it, the sun shone down, illuminating the room in a paradisiacal glow that felt warm. The smell of lavender and sandalwood cut through the damp, musky smell of the cave. The urge to sit by the fall forever grew paramount.

I let my eyes wander the room, forgetting where I was for only a moment before I saw the beings that had befriended Riley standing in the water at the base of the waterfall. They were gathered in a circle with their arm-like limbs entangled, the body of her friend floating in the middle. There was a low humming that seemed to be coming from the beings, though none of their mouths seemed to be moving in any discernible way.

I stepped closer to them, hoping to get a better idea as to what this ceremony was. It felt spiritual. It felt private. My boot struck a loose stone, and the being facing my direction rose its head and stared at me. I was no longer scared of them. In fact, here, in the warm light of the sun, standing at the base of beauty, I saw why Riley cared so much for them. They were serene, pure, and beautiful.

The one that had seen me lowered its head once more, and the humming noise got louder, threatening to drown out the sound of the waterfall in totality. I watched in awe as the body of Riley's friend sank below the surface of the water, and a translucent light rose above. The light hovered for a few moments before drifting over the heads of each of the beings in the circle. The light shone brighter over each head before rising high above and disappearing into the sunlight.

I found the experience to be moving beyond words. I was only slightly aware of the tears streaming from my eyes as the beings released their entanglement and turned to face me. The one that had seen me previously stepped toward me and placed its hands upon my shoulders, staring deeply into my eyes, seeing all of me.

It made a quick, deep hum and nodded its head. It stepped back from me and pointed in the distance, away from the waterfall. I turned my head, allowing the headlamp to illuminate the area in which it was pointing, and saw another dark hall. Unlike the previous halls, my light refused to penetrate the inky void.

I looked back at the being in front of me and asked, "She's there, isn't she?"

It nodded and once more took a step forward and put its hands against my temples. An image of Riley filled my sight. She was sitting in a darkened corner down there. Her knees were pulled up to her chest and she was rocking back and forth. Her eyes cast down and hidden, her fear, even in this vision, was palpable.

The being released its touch and stepped back once more. Simultaneously, the several still standing at the base of the waterfall, and the one before me, placed their right hands against the front of their heads and bowed low. Though I didn't understand their language, I knew what they were saying.

Good luck.

"I don't know if you can understand me, but thank you," I said in deference.

With no more time to spare, I headed off into the blackness that held Riley. Toward the beast's realm.

Hours passed by. Hell, maybe days passed by. It was impossible to tell in a world lit only by the light strapped to my head. My ears rang with the thundering silence I found myself immersed in. Occasionally, my foot would kick a loose rock that crossed my path, or trickles of water would be heard in the cracks of the rocks around me, but with those few exceptions, utter silence reigned.

And it was getting hot. At first, I thought it was some sort of an illusion that my brain was concocting. The air was feeling heavier the deeper I walked. Perhaps I was exerting so much energy that my body was unable to keep itself cool. What was once comfortable soon became balmy and then oppressive.

Sweat poured from my head, causing the strap of the headlamp to slide down—several times—in front of my eyes. My shirt clung to my back and chest but still, I pressed on.

My heart froze when I stopped walking immediately before my foot would have come down on nothing but open air. A loose rock went over the edge, and I counted at least four seconds before I heard it land below. A straight drop with no way around.

A hot breeze floated up from the depths, bringing a sulfuric smell that made me back away, my bilious stomach causing me to lean up against the cave wall. I had no idea what to do. There was no way around it, and the drop was a death trap. *Then again,* I thought, *I'm already dying.*

I edged myself to the lip of the drop and stared down, holding my breath so as to not give in to the nausea that threatened. My light shone brightly, but I could see no bottom. The hot breeze blowing up at me signaled danger, but it also signaled my way forward. The beings had pointed me down this tunnel. This was the way.

As I looked away from the precipitous drop and focused on the walls leading down, I saw little handholds jutting out. I chanced a breath through my mouth and out my nose, not quite as bad as the opposite.

Just like the climb down to the waterfall, Matt. Nothing different than before. Just like the ladders. Go slowly, find your holds, and you'll make it.

I made myself believe this. I willed myself to trust in my ability. She was at the bottom of this chasm. I was sure of it. As I sat and let my legs dangle over the edge, I gathered the remaining courage I had. Riley's energy, Riley's eternal being hung in the balance.

I turned onto my stomach and let my right foot find the first hold. "Just move deliberately, Matt," I said into the darkness.

One foot at a time, I made my way down into the depths of the underworld.

When I finally reached the bottom, I had to take a moment for my entire body to stop shaking. The adrenaline coursing through me made me feel invincible and yet unable to stand firm on my own two legs. I decided to take a moment and sit, giving them a rest at the base of what I had just scaled. The smell was putrid down here. It made my head dizzy, though I told myself it was nothing more than the exertion of climbing down. I'd be better after just a few minutes.

The hot breeze plagued me as I tried to relax, but it brought with it something that I didn't fully expect. The soft whimper of a child hidden somewhere in the devastating darkness.

"Riley? Where are you?"

Silence.

"Riley, talk to me!"

I willed my legs to work and stood. I took a step forward, and her scream cut through the shadows. "Dad, it's here! Help m—" Her voice was abruptly cut off, and fear gripped every fiber of my being.

I ran. As dangerous as it was to do so with no more than a headlamp to guide me, I ran faster than I had ever run before. I willed myself forward into the inky-dark world with no care for my own safety. My only goal was to find her. To find Riley.

I suddenly found myself in a room that towered above. A small source of light illuminated the ceiling of this cavern, but only a small portion of that light was able to reach the floor where I stood with my hands on my knees, searching.

I turned behind me and saw her sitting in the corner, her head buried against her knees, torn arms holding herself in a tight hug.

"Riley, I'm here." I ran to her and placed my hands on her shoulders. She screamed, horrified that the beast had returned to do her more harm. "No, Riley, it's me, Dad. I'm here. I've got you."

She looked up at me, one eye swelled shut, a bruise forming around her left cheek. "Dad, you came for me."

I pulled her close to me, unaware of any pain that I may be causing by squeezing her so tight. "Yes, baby. I came for you. Let's get out of here now, huh?"

I felt her head nodding against my chest, then I felt her head rise, her eyes looking high above. She pushed back slowly, never taking her eyes off the ceiling. "Dad…"

I turned and pointed my headlamp up, but there was no need. In the light that shone above, the beast hovered, its leathery wings flapping slowly, its massive body battered and torn from the battle with the beings in the swamp.

"Riley, stay back. Just stay right there."

The beast lowered itself out of the light and into the darkness. The beam from my lamp followed it down until its cloven feet touched down. I hadn't seen the creature on the ground this close to me before. It was huge. It must have been two feet taller than I was. Its muscles rippled under its shredded flesh. Its wings were torn in places, but they had still been strong enough to hold it above with ease.

It stood no more than six feet from me, but it wouldn't stare into my eyes. *The light,* I thought. I stepped forward brazenly. "Whatever you are, you need to leave us alone!" I screamed at the beast.

A deep growl bellowed throughout the room as it raised its face directly into the beam of light. An inhuman voice rumbled forth as it raised its clawed hand in the direction of Riley. "**Mine.**"

The beast lunged toward her. With a reaction time I didn't realize I had, I dove in front of it. It slammed into me with the power of a freight train. I couldn't tell if I had blacked out because of the darkness—my headlamp now lying to my right, shining against the wall farthest away from me.

I felt shattered. My eyes tried to focus on the lamp, but they couldn't. I felt a warm trickle of what I knew must be blood dripping down the backside of my neck. I couldn't feel my legs, and there was something sharp digging into my back.

It was over. I had failed her. The beast had us both exactly where it wanted us. My eyes began to close, and I started to drift away. I felt myself leaving the room. The esoteric feeling of leaving one's body while being aware that you are not exactly *in* your body is something I can't fully explain, but suffice it to say, I was losing my grip on that place.

With the last flickers of awareness, I saw myself running through the woods. I was scared, utterly terrified. The trees were opening and closing in on each other all around me. I had the sudden realization that, in this place, I was able to manipulate the environment. My energy wasn't constrained by the bounds of physics and Earth because I wasn't *on* Earth. At least, the Earth in which I was raised. I slowly felt myself becoming more aware, though the vision of running through the woods was still prominent before me.

Then, without warning, I was struck by the moose that had sent me flying against the massive tree days ago. I lay at the base of the tree, not feeling my body but feeling that damn root digging into my back. I saw myself testing my toes and my fingers. I saw myself move and realize that I wasn't hurt.

Then I saw the beam of light from my headlamp be cut as the beast walked in front of it.

I shifted slowly, getting the damn pointy stone out of my back. I tested my toes and my fingers. I heard the sound of the sharp stone tearing from the wall and landing behind me as I shifted. The beast's heavy footsteps stopped, and I froze in place.

I held my breath for what felt like an eternity before I heard the footsteps continue and the soft cries from Riley begin in kind. *She must have run when I got in front of the creature. She tried to hide on the other side of the room.*

Quietly, I rose, unsure of what I was going to do but knowing that I needed to do it quickly.

"Don't let fear rule you. Look at your situation and find the solution," my father's voice echoed in my mind.

I stepped forward toward the beast when my foot lightly struck something. When I reached down and grabbed it, I realized it was the sharp stone that had fallen from the cave wall. Its sharp tip would work. It was all I had; it would have to be enough.

I could see the beast's feet as they stayed in the light. I crept slowly behind it, making sure every step was deliberate but moving with as much haste as I could safely allow. As I got within striking distance, I watched as the shadowy shoulders of the massive creature rose and fell with each breath. The sulfuric smell mashed against my nostrils as I took my place behind it.

The beast bent over, and Riley screamed. I used the stone as a knife and tore the length of the already damaged wings. The beast rose with a yell and turned toward me, swinging its claws in the dark, ready to take my head off. Instinctually, I ducked and felt the breeze from its mighty arm pass over me. I gripped the stone tightly and came up fast and hard, driving the pointed end of the stone through the underside of the beast's jaw.

Nothing moved inside that cavern for several seconds when, abruptly, the beast fell to its knees and then onto its stomach. The bloody pool of blackened gore shone in the beam from the headlamp.

I collapsed onto my knees and was immediately tackled to the ground by Riley. Her arms wrapped tight around my neck, and she wept. "Thank you, Dad. Thank you."

I caressed her head and noted the tangles of her hair. The sulfur smell started to dissipate, and the smell of lavender and sandalwood flooded my nostrils. My eyes were heavy, and keeping them open became nearly impossible.

As I was about to give in to the rest that called to me, I noticed the darkness of the room began to take on a red hue. A dark red circle began to fully encompass the beast's body, and suddenly, the floor around it opened up. The beast must have fallen through eternity because I never heard its body land.

I let my eyes fall shut. Riley's rhythmic breathing signaling that she had succumbed to exhaustion as well.

With the last moments of awareness that I had inside that cave, I felt myself being carried upward.

Up toward the light.

Chapter 23

I awoke with the sun in my eyes once more. The grass underneath me cushioned my sore body. Sore but not broken. The trees were bare of almost all their leaves now, and there was an aura of change all around me.

I heard whispering behind me, and I turned to see Riley and my father talking to several of the tree beings that, I had assumed, carried us out of the darkness and back into the light. Their conversation seemed to be of paramount importance as each of their stern, worried faces conveyed the tone of the conversation that I could not hear. When they turned to look at me, their discussion abruptly ended, and Riley ran to me, throwing her arms around me.

"You're awake!" she gleefully squealed into my chest.

I sat up slowly, keeping an arm around her as I did so. "I'm awake."

The tree beings walked over to Riley and me, encircling us. As their tree-like limbs entangled together, the soft, deep humming sound that I had become familiar with began in full. The air around us seemed to reverberate slightly as they rocked side to side.

"What are they doing?" I asked as I watched them, awestruck.

Riley lifted her head and looked at them knowingly. "They're saying goodbye."

"Goodbye?"

"Yes, you have a decision to make now. But, whatever that decision is, you won't be *here* anymore."

I looked around to find my father, who was slowly making his way into the circle that had formed around us. I rose to my feet, Riley grasping my hand and holding it tightly against her face. My father's stolid face gave away no thoughts, only resoluteness. He stepped a few feet in front of me and reached out, clasping my shoulders once more.

"Matt, you did it. You've learned to overcome your fear. You didn't let your anxiety toward a seemingly impossible task get in the way. I'm so proud of you." He embraced me tightly, his arms squeezing me so close that I thought, in this place, we might meld together as one.

When he stepped back, I spoke. "That…thing—"

"Is gone, for now. It was here for Riley. It sensed her pure energy and craved it. You sent it back to where it came from. It will be back again, not now, but sometime. But, by then, we'll be long gone, too."

"Where will you go?"

"Well, I guess that depends on your decision." The low humming continued somewhere in the back of my mind as my head swam. I felt hypnotized. Something was happening.

"My decision?"

My father nodded, and Riley pulled herself closer to me once more. "Will you stay with us, or will you go back to your body? To Jane and Laura?"

The sun felt warm on my face. The air, crisp in my lungs. The soft touch of Riley's face against my hand pulled my heart to this place.

"I…I can't leave, Dad. How can I?"

"Mhmm, truly, it's a difficult choice. But, it is a choice you must make by yourself. I can't help you make it."

I looked down at my daughter, clutching my hand to her face, desperately not wanting to let go. I stared into my father's eyes, and a tear spilled from my own as I contemplated the consequences of my choice.

The soft whimpering of a child echoed in my mind, but I realized it wasn't Riley. It was Laura. Somewhere far away, in another place and time, she called to me. I realized I could sense her fear even from the other side of eternity. Then I heard the loud bang of the gun going off and the pain of the bullet entering my gut. The searing heat as it tore through layers of skin and muscle. Laura's cries went silent.

"What happens if I stay?"

"Well," my father considered, "you'll go with us to the other place. You'll—"

"No," I interjected. "What happens to them? To Laura and Jane."

"Oh." My father paused and lowered his eyes, unable to look into mine when he spoke, "Unbearable pain, Matt."

The blow to my heart was almost worse than the bullet to my stomach. I lurched forward and sobbed.

"Dad, it's okay. We're here. We're here with you." Riley kissed my cheek softly before pulling my head to her shoulder. My child, young as she was, consoling me in the way in which I should have been consoling her. Whatever decision I made would affect her, too. Her form may not be physical, but being in that place was as real as that dark alley behind *Yummy Burger*. I slowly sucked air through my teeth and rose again.

"And, if I go back? You'll both be gone forever?"

The hint of a smile crossed my father's face. "Not forever. For a time, yes. A time that will feel longer to you than to us, but we will be here, watching from afar."

My breath caught as the clarity of my choice came to me. I looked down at Riley and smiled. She returned mine with one of her own as tears flowed down her cheeks. I could see that she was trying to control her breathing, trying to be strong, but even in this place, her energy was too young to hide the torrent of emotions that peeked out behind her eyes.

"You're going, aren't you?"

My heart shattered. "Riley, I have to. Your mom…your sister… they are in trouble."

"And you have to save them. Like you saved me?"

I nodded and knelt in front of her. We had been through so much in such a short amount of time that it felt wrong to leave her. Yet, necessary. This place had something to show me, something that I had to learn, and learn, I did. Riley had guided me—she was my guardian angel if an agnostic like myself could use such a term. My father was the light that guided me through my physical life. Riley was the light that guided my energy here.

I had realized that walking my way through life, avoiding all risks, all things that were *scary,* was to only embrace part of my time on earth. Riley showed me that just waking up each day was a risk in itself. My father had given me the words to hold onto, and Riley had given me the push that I needed to heed them.

"Yes." The whispered word hung in the air in front of us. The humming from the forest creatures slowly faded, and I turned to see that where they once stood were trees. Solid trees that stood lower than those surrounding us but taller than my father and I at our full height. The forest was silent now. My decision had been made.

I turned back and saw that Riley's tears had faded, and her smile shone as bright as the sun above. "I was right. You were ready for what was next." She stood up and grabbed my father's hand as he walked up next to me. "See, Grandpa, he's going to be alright."

My father looked at me and pulled me close to him. "Yes," he said into my ear, "I believe you're going to be alright, Matt."

My frenzied tears flowed, and I let them. As the moments passed, I felt a tug on my energy. Not a physical tug, but an ethereal one, beckoning me back to my body. The pain in my stomach came back steadily, and I was compelled to push away from my father's grasp. The vivid world around me began to blur and fade slowly.

As the world I had known for the past several days disappeared, I saw two figures, one smaller than the other, holding hands in front of me. The world rapidly became an oil painting before my eyes as the pain threatened to take over. And, amongst the swirling colors fighting off the oncoming darkness, I heard the last words I'd ever hear from my unborn daughter.

"I love you, Dad."

Chapter 24

I woke with a start, but thankfully, not a loud gasp of breath. The cold pavement, covered with ice and snow, was disorienting, so I pressed my eyes closed tightly, trying to regain a sense of control against my swirling mind.

Her voice still echoed in my head. "I love you, Dad."

My heart ached to hold her again. Deep down, I knew that I had held my unborn daughter for the last time. I knew that I wouldn't hear her voice again. I knew I wouldn't see her smile. Visions of our adventure through the woods played behind my closed eyelids as I desperately tried to hold onto the fading memories of the last few days.

Or was it only the last few minutes?

Suddenly, the sound of whimpering cut through my daze, and my eyes snapped open once more. My stomach screamed with white-hot pain, and my hands were frozen over the throbbing hole that still spewed warm blood. I could feel my fingers slipping against each other, all the while getting stickier by the moment.

The whimpering continued and then the muffled sound of a woman screaming with something over her mouth caused me to cautiously move my head to get a look at the scene. I could only just make out the small, curled-up figure pressed up against the side of the building, hiding in the shadows, desperate to not be seen but failing to stay silent. I could also see a man pressing my wife against the brick building behind the burger joint. The gun moved to her temple, his hand covering her mouth, his hips moving in a rhythmic way against her that made my skin crawl.

"Ah, you *bitch*!" he screamed as he pulled his hand away, shaking it violently.

It was clear that Jane had bitten him—and bit him hard, considering his reaction. Even in the face of certain death, she fought back. *That's my girl*, I thought as the world came back clearer by the moment.

She turned around to face him just as he was done shaking his hand. Even in the darkness, I could feel the hatred radiating off his body. With one swift motion, in the same instant that Jane turned to face him, his fist connected against her jaw. Jane dropped like a sack of bricks.

Laura got to her feet at the moment that my feet slowly started to find footing. I moved slowly, not just to not startle this maniac but because my brain was only just starting to remember how to move my body.

Laura ran with all the force she could muster and slammed her fists into the man's stomach. *That's my girl.*

Even with all her anger, with all the force she could muster, he was just too big and strong. He looked down at her and grabbed a fistful of her hair. Laura screamed, and I slowly rolled to the side, the man's back now to where I lay.

"Let go of me, you creep. Just *STOP!*" she screamed at the top of her lungs. I saw a figure at the other end of the alley step around the corner and then disappear back from where it came from, its hand held to its face.

"Just sit over there, brat. I'll deal with you next." He shoved her hard against the brick wall, and I heard a smack as Laura's head connected. She slid down the wall slowly, holding her head. A good sign, I thought, that she was aware enough to grab her head and ease herself down rather than just collapse into a heap.

I flexed my fingers and cautiously moved them away from my wound. I needed to be sure they still worked for what came next. The man moved quickly and grabbed Jane by her hair, her limp body his to do what he would. He never looked over in my direction, and why would he, I thought. For all he knew, I was dead. I realized if I could just get my limbs to work the way I wanted to, I could stop this madness.

When he lifted Jane, she seemed to regain some level of consciousness. Her legs were wobbly but somewhat able to hold her weight as he steadied her. He dragged her to the dumpster and pressed his knee against her lower back, keeping her standing while he fumbled with his belt.

If I was going to stop this situation, it *had* to be now. I sucked a deep breath in and held onto it as I forced myself to a sitting position. The pain radiated from the hole in my stomach like ripples on a calm lake, but I pushed through it.

I slowly got to my feet, careful not to stand too quickly and risk falling back to the ground. Not only would I be no help there, but the noise would surely startle the man into the realization that I was not dead. And then, I was sure I would be.

For a moment, my heart sank as my vision tunneled, and I wavered, but it passed just as quickly as it came, and I was steady.

Now what?

The man was still fumbling with his belt when I took my first step forward. Panic rose inside me as my mind flashed back to the loud bang and the flash of light, and my stomach throbbed in response.

Look at your situation and find the solution.

My dad's voice rang in my head like a lighthouse beam showing the way to sailors in the dark. My eyes focused on a brick lying just to my right, and I knew what I would do. Unwilling to acknowledge the pain any longer, I bent down and picked it up just as the man's pants fell to his knees. Jane groaned as realization snuck into her brain, and Laura whimpered in the darkness once more.

I gripped the brick tightly, its pointed ridges digging into my palm. The stickiness of the blood on my hand held it firmly in place as I threw all caution to the wind and ran forward. By my second step, the man turned and faced me, his gun pointed back in my direction. By my third, the brick was shattering between my bloody palm and his crushed nose.

I heard the sound of metal against the ground as the man's hands went to his face. He dropped to his knees, screaming, and dared to look up to my eyes. At that moment, rage filled me. Rage that had brewed within since I heard what he had done to Sarah. Rage for what he was going to do to Laura. Rage for what he was about to do to Jane.

I drove my knee directly into his disfigured face. His hands may have deflected some of the blow, but the force with which his head slammed against the dumpster told me that it hadn't deflected too much. Jane stumbled to the side semi-consciously, and the man fell to the ground.

There was no more pain in my stomach. No more dizziness to be cautiously aware of. There was only hate. I kicked the man against the dumpster over and over. I kicked him until my legs were weary. I kicked him until my lungs couldn't suck any more air.

I kicked him until I felt a soft pull on my hand. I looked down and saw Laura, tears in her eyes, mouthing words that I could not make out through the fog of rage that had overtaken me. I stared at her, my adrenaline ebbing quickly. Her voice rose from the depths like a buoy, bringing me back to reality.

"Dad, stop. We're okay now."

On the brick wall in front of me, I saw red and blue lights flashing. I heard tires screeching and shouting. At that moment, my legs gave out, and I once again collapsed onto the cold ground. Jane stumbled over to my prone body, and Laura wrapped her arms around my neck. The warmth grew from within and radiated off of my body. I was back; I had saved them.

In the next moment, I was being flipped over onto my stomach roughly by an officer who was forcing my hands behind my back. The cuffs were cold against me as the warmth of my wife and daughter faded without their touch.

I heard Jane screaming at the officer that I was her husband and innocent. That the man on the ground had assaulted her and our daughter and that I had saved them.

As I lay there, cold and getting colder as the blood pooled beneath me, I smiled.

They were going to be okay.

Chapter 25

The sharp pinpricks that signaled that my legs had gone completely numb rose from my toes to my knee. The late afternoon sun streamed through the windows as the man who had called to inquire about an interview several weeks ago closed his computer and sighed deeply. He removed the glasses from his face and pinched his thumb and pointer finger across the bridge of his nose.

"Wow, Mr. Burke. That's an incredible story."

I shook my head as I repositioned myself on the bed, careful not to pinch any of the tubes that ran from my arm into the machine that beeped monotonously behind me. "Not a story, Mr. Stone. Just the truth as accurate as this old mind can remember."

My hospital room door opened, and Laura walked in with a bag that smelled like last night's leftovers, much better than the food the hospital offered. She had been coming to the hospital for the past two weeks since I had what the doctors called a mild heart attack. I don't know what's mild about any heart attack, but it seemed to give her comfort hearing the doctors describe it as such. With Jane passing last year of her own heart attack, though hers a massive one, it's no wonder Laura is by my side as often as she can be.

"Mrs. Page, I'm glad to see you again," the man with the glasses now placed securely on the bridge of his nose said. As he rose, placing his laptop on the ground, he offered his chair to Laura.

"Hi, sweetheart," I said as I reached, slowly, toward the meal.

"Hi, Dad." She leaned down and kissed my cheek.

The years had been kind to Laura, physically. She had so far been able to avoid the heart conditions that seemed to want to put an end to both her parents. She had just passed her fiftieth birthday, although she looked at least a decade younger, and her smile still lit up any room she entered.

"How's he doing today?" she asked the interviewer.

"Docs were in here an hour or so ago. Said he seemed fine."

I saw her nod with acceptance, seeing the same thing in his eyes that I knew myself.

"Ah, Christ, Joe, tell the girl the truth." My eyes centered on Laura's, and I saw the pain hidden just behind the surface. "It's not looking good, sweetheart."

"Wh-what do you mean? What did the doctor say?"

I struggle to keep my hands from showing the strain of simply lifting the to-go container of food that she brought me. I can't believe how weak I've gotten in the last few days.

I sigh deeply, more to try to fill my lungs with air than in frustration from the question. "The old ticker is getting weaker. Weaker than yesterday. Weaker than the day before." I shrug, having resigned myself to the prognosis, only becoming aware of the callousness of it all when I see Laura's tears boil over. "Sweetheart, I'm sorry…"

She holds up a hand and wipes away the tears. Joe looks uncomfortable and rubs the back of his head as he walks to the back of the room. "Dad, I understand. It's different to be going through it on your end than it is to be going through it on mine." She forces a smile, and her strength fills me, at least momentarily, with some of my own.

I reach for her hand and motion for her to sit on the bed next to me. When I call out to Joe, he turns slowly, guilt pronounced on his face.

"Don't look so damn solemn, Joe."

"Sorry, Mr. Burke. It's just, you know, I feel like I've gotten to know you over the last few days, and, well, I'm feeling guilty. Having you dredge up all this difficult-to-process stuff. And, with your heart being weak as it is—"

Now it's my turn to hold up my hand. "Joe, I'm the one that responded to your post."

"Ah—" Laura corrects.

"Laura is the one that answered your post." I turn to Laura again. "But only because I asked you to." When I turn back to Joe, his hand is on the back of the chair. "Now, will you sit down and finish asking your questions? I'm getting pretty tired. I want to be sure you have it all for this book of yours."

With a soft smile and perhaps the slightest bit of reluctance, he sat and placed his laptop back in his lap.

As Laura made to move off the bed and likely head back into the hallway, I squeezed her hand a little tighter. "Stay, please."

Her eyes danced across my face, and she paled slightly. "Okay, Dad."

I smiled at her and turned back, ready to answer anything else he'd ask. With as much strength in my voice as I could muster, "What else do you want to know?"

Joe scrolled through the notes he had taken and nodded every few seconds as he processed the information that I had told him.

"Well, Mr. Burke, this story...well, this story is amazing. I think we're going to have a real hit here." He smiled brightly, and I forced my own. "I think the only thing I have left to ask is, what happened after that night in the alley? What did the rest of your life bring to you?"

Visions filled my mind, watching Laura grow up; the birthday parties, the sleepovers, the family trips, and the memories we shared together. My granddaughter, graduating college next year, her fiance, and the home they had already started to build together. The Thanksgiving dinners and the Christmas mornings. The laughter. The tears.

Jane.

My love. The love I knew the instant I had seen her in my classroom that day. The adventures we planned and never took. The quiet nights at home, her head resting on my shoulder as I flipped through a book. I swear I can smell her perfume even at this moment. The candlelight dinners and the crackling of the fireplace. Her voice whispering softly into my ear, telling me the secrets of her soul.

My eyes drift to the corner of the room, and I smile. The memories come flooding back, and I drink them in with an unquenchable thirst.

"The rest of my life," I say in a voice barely above a whisper. "The rest of my life brought me nothing but the utmost joy and happiness." I can feel my heart throbbing so hard it's almost painful; Laura squeezes my hand softly.

"I'm sorry, Mr. Stone. I think I'll have to ask you to leave now. I'm getting really tired, and I'd like to spend a few moments with my daughter before I rest."

He stands up and thanks me for the story. He promises to tell it just as I had. It will be the main story in his book on near-death experiences. I thank him for his time and wish him the best. *He's a good man*, I think. *He will tell the story true.*

Laura closes the door behind him and comes back to sit by my side. My heart is getting weaker now. The recounting of the story, the memories of what I've seen, finally seem to have caught up to me.

"Dad," she says as she chokes back tears. "Dad, are you okay?"

I look at Laura, and I think that I've never been better. "You've grown up to be such an amazing woman, Laura. You've made me prouder than I'll ever be able to tell you."

A single tear flows down over the curve of her cheek and falls onto our hands, clasped together in oneness.

"And you've made me proud, Dad. That night…behind the burger place—"

"Shh," I beg. "No need to think about that now. It was a lifetime ago, and whatever pain we all felt that night has long been washed away. Stay with me now, and think of the beauty of the world. Not the ugliness."

I let my eyes drift back to the corner of the room. My father and mother are standing hand-in-hand, smiling at me. They are young, beautiful, and real. As real as the bed I'm lying in. As real as Laura's hand holding mine. My eyes get misty, but I blink it away, desperate to look at them longer. The aura of their love starts in the corner of the room, a variegated prism that reaches toward me in slow motion.

"You see them, don't you?"

I let my eyes pull away to look back at Laura. Her brow furrowed as she tries to maintain composure. Knowing that, no matter how tight she holds my hand, I'm fading from her. With all the strength I have remaining, I pull her hand to my lips.

"I love you, Laura."

I look back to the corner and see her standing there, smiling that beautiful smile I had seen so long ago. Riley steps out of the prismatic light that is still stretching toward me and reaches her arm to me. She hasn't aged a moment. She turns toward the light again and mouths words that I can't hear. When she turns back to me, I realize what she was saying. Jane steps out and takes Riley's outstretched hand. Jane, looking as she did the moment I saw her for the first time.

They close the distance between us quicker now. My breath growing shallow and ragged. I blink slowly as the blinding aura of peace and beauty covers me. The colors flow over me like the autumn leaves of my youth, falling all around me.

"I love you so much, Dad," Laura whispers as she kisses the hand she has held.

Riley takes one final step and reaches out for my loose hand. She grabs it and squeezes tight. Her smile blotting out the colors above.

Author's Note

The bones of the story that became *Beyond the Autumn Leaves* were dug up almost simultaneously with the concept for my debut novel, *Isolation*. After writing the short story that later became *Isolation* (chapter 35), I found myself drawn to what I had with *BTAL*. I knew that I had to write this novel in first-person perspective, a challenge I hadn't undertaken in any of my previous writing–published or unpublished. I quickly discovered the difficulty in doing this and temporarily shelved this project to complete *Isolation*, knowing full well that Matt and Riley's story was only on a temporary hiatus.

While I had a bit of difficulty writing in first-person (it is a challenge I'd like to take up again in the future), I decided that I would have fun with the novel and utilize my favorite literary device—symbolism. Those readers with a keen eye may have recognized the changing of color in Matt's tent or that the animals he encounters seem to stand out in certain scenes. This was done in an attempt to set the mood and, in some cases, explain in further subtle detail what Matt was experiencing.

There are also some "Easter Eggs" in *BTAL* that close readers may find relating to *Isolation* and some upcoming works that I am unable to currently divulge too much information on. Suffice it to say, it is a fun exercise for me to place words, phrases, or descriptions that harken back to other work or illustrate what is to come in my future works. Keep an eye out for these in any story I write.

This story is close to my heart as there is a large focus on the father-daughter relationship. Since becoming a father eighteen years ago, I've become a bit of a sap, tearing up or sobbing at the first sign of a father's conflict with his children. Writing *BTAL* hit me straight in the heart several times, and I'm not afraid to say I teared up more than once (I hope some of you felt the same way).

Aside from my exploration of father-daughter (or father-son relationships should you want to extrapolate the story and place a son in the role of Riley, a non-gender-specific name chosen for that reason—also my daughter's middle name) relationships, Matt's relationship with his father mirrors, in some ways, my own relationship with my father. While John Grace would have never gone out and hiked the mountains, I illustrate in this story, the care, love, and guidance that Matt's father shows, I believe, reflects some of my experiences with my father.

Lastly, while some of the mountains in the story are real (Mount Morgan, Mount Percival, etc.) Mount Whitehorse is not a peak that exists in New Hampshire. It is, in fact, named after Whitehorse Ledge in North Conway, NH—one of my favorite places to visit in New England.

When describing the Alpine Staircase, I was reflecting on one of my first "real" hikes in New Hampshire: Mount Tecumseh. Hiking Mount Tecumseh was incredibly easy initially and then rapidly becomes a staircase that seems to never want to end as you climb, and climb, and climb some more. If you ever come to New Hampshire or have been in the past, the region where Mount Whitehorse is situated would be just past Franconia Notch, where the Old Man has reigned prominently.

About the Author

Jared Grace is the author of *Isolation*, his well-received debut horror novel that's already making waves as a finalist for the Indie Ink Awards 2024 in various categories. Born just south of Boston, Massachusetts, Jared now calls the scenic White Mountains of New Hampshire home, where he spends his days hiking trails, chasing his muse, researching paranormal events, and devouring books from his favorite authors across a wide range of genres.

When he's not working on his next spine-tingling tale, Jared is a proud dad to his two incredible kids, Jordan and Wyatt, who keep him equally terrified and inspired (but in the best way).

After a brief pit stop at Boston College, Jared earned not one but two bachelor's degrees—English and history—from Southern New Hampshire University in 2014.

Jared's love for history, nature, travel, and the supernatural seeps into his stories, making them equal parts eerie, thought-provoking, and unputdownable. Whether he's digging into spooky folklore or climbing a mountain, Jared finds inspiration everywhere—especially in the things that go bump in the night.